'C[...]

There was a rust[...]
around Hassan. [...]
now.'

Hassan opened his eyes and then immediately closed them again, unable to believe what he was seeing. He felt as if he'd been catapulted into a fantasy.

Cautiously he opened his eyes again. Nothing had changed. Kali was still wearing a provocative costume consisting of long filmy blue scarves and glittering sliver sequins.

'Isn't this outfit spectacular? I bought it from the woman who gave the belly dancing demonstration. Belly dancing raises the heart rate satisfactorily,' she murmured, leaning towards him.

'Heart rate?' he repeated distractedly as she began to move her hips in an undulating movement.

'Oh, yes. Belly dancing is marvellous for your heart.' The husky whisper rasped over his nerve endings. Hassan felt as if he were about to plunge into an abyss of sexual desire that would wholly consume him.

Dear Reader,

Welcome to August's offering of Desires! This month we bring you an incredibly sexy MAN OF THE MONTH, Flint Paradise in Barbara Boswell's *Forever Flint*. How will he react when he finds out lover Ashlinn Carey is pregnant?

We begin a new mini-series this month—THE MILLIONAIRE'S CLUB. Five special, wealthy men find true love and happiness while on a secret mission. Dixie Browning's first up with *Texas Millionaire*. And we've got the second in Cathie Linz's trilogy THE MARRIAGE MAKERS, *Too Stubborn To Marry*—Ryan Knight knows who he wants, but how's he going to get her?

There's a sheikh pretending to be someone he's not in Judith McWilliams's *The Sheikh's Secret*. And old friends become lovers in *Kiss Your Prince Charming*. Finally, Anne Eames brings us *The Unknown Malone*—Michael Phillips realises there's more to single mother Nicole Bedder than meets the eye...

Enjoy them all,

The Editors

The Sheikh's Secret

JUDITH McWILLIAMS

SILHOUETTE

DESIRE

*First published in Great Britain 2000
Silhouette Books, Eton House, 18-24 Paradise Road,
Richmond, Surrey TW9 1SR*

© Judith McWilliams 1999

ISBN 0 373 76228 3

22-0008

*Printed and bound in Spain
by Litografía Rosés S.A., Barcelona*

JUDITH McWILLIAMS

began to enjoy romances while in search of the proverbial 'happily ever after'. But she always found herself
rewriting the endings, and eventually the beginnings, of
the books she read. Her husband finally suggested that
she write novels of her own, and she's been doing so
ever since. An ex-teacher with four children, Judith has
travelled the country extensively with her husband and
has been greatly influenced by those experiences. But
while not tending the garden or caring for family,
Judith does what she enjoys most—writing. She has
also written under the name Charlotte Hines.

One

Hassan Rashid reluctantly crossed the small lobby of Kali Whitman's apartment building, double-checked the apartment which Karim had given him, then slowly pushed the call button beside the elevator.

Maybe his brother would be right for once in his life, Hassan thought, encouraging himself. Maybe this Kali Whitman really wouldn't care when he told her that Karim was breaking their engagement.

"Yes?"

The musical lilt of the softly feminine voice that emerged from the call box poured through Hassan, raising both his body temperature and his doubts about the whole situation. That voice certainly didn't sound as if it belonged to a cold woman who had agreed to trade romance for a marriage of convenience.

But then, who better than he knew that appearances were quite often deceptive. Physically he was the mirror image of Karim and yet, mentally, they were poles apart. Karim was an extrovert, the life and soul of every social gathering, while he was far more reserved. Social chit-chat did not come easily to him.

"Is anyone there?" Kali's voice sharpened slightly, and Hassan hurriedly cut off his thoughts. He didn't want her annoyed to start with. She was going to be upset enough once he broke the news of Karim's perfidy to her.

"Sorry," he began.

"Karim! Thank heavens you're back. Come on up. I need to talk to you."

Damn! Hassan thought. Karim was wrong. Again.

Kali's welcome hadn't been that of a woman who didn't care one way or the other about her engagement. She was clearly ecstatic to hear her fiancé's voice. As if she'd been counting the days until Karim returned to New York.

But why? Hassan wondered uncertainly. According to Karim, their engagement was an arranged affair based on their mutual respect for each other's work with emotionally troubled children rather than any personal feelings they had for each other. He'd said that they had met during the course of their work and had never actually dated.

Karim had told him that he'd felt it was time he married and had children, and he'd decided that he'd have a better chance of making a success of marriage if he chose a woman who shared his interests and goals. That, when he'd made a list of the women he knew, he'd realized that Kali Whitman fit all his requirements for a wife. So he'd written her a letter explaining his position and asking her to marry him. Karim had said that she had considered his proposal for almost a week before finally accepting it the day before he'd had to fly to Australia for a conference.

Hassan frowned. Of course Karim's assumption that her acceptance meant that she agreed with his practical approach to marriage didn't mean it was true. Kali Whitman could have agreed to marry his brother because she was in love with him.

He had no way of knowing what her original motivation had been, and he hated walking into a situation blind.

Hassan forced himself to enter the elevator when his every instinct was urging him to run from what threatened to be a very unpleasant interview. But he couldn't. He was the responsible twin, he reminded himself. The twin who had always tried to make amends for Karim's thoughtless behavior. But this was the last time! From now on, Karim could clean up his own messes.

The elevator slid to a smooth stop on the sixth floor.

Hassan stepped out and headed toward 6C, still undecided as to how to tell her what Karim had done.

Stopping in front of Kali's apartment, he stared blindly at the oak door. Maybe the best way to break the news would be a blunt, unemotional statement of the facts. But the problem was it wouldn't stay unemotional for long. She'd probably burst into tears and then what was he supposed to do?

He shifted uncomfortably at the thought of trying to deal with a hysterical woman.

He lifted his hand to knock, but before he could, the door swung open.

Hassan blinked, his hand suspended in midair as he stared at the unexpected vision in front of him. Small and slender, Kali barely reached his chin. He swallowed uneasily as he noticed the thrust of her full breasts against the rust-colored sweater she was wearing. Hastily wrenching his gaze upward, he turned his attention to the cloud of reddish-brown hair that framed the creamy perfection of her ivory skin and the delicacy of her perfectly formed features.

The strangest sense of disorientation filled him when his eyes met hers. They were the most gorgeous color, like the chestnuts that grew on his mother's estate in England.

Chestnuts were good luck, his nanny had told him. As a boy he'd gathered them by the pocketfuls and hidden them in his room against future need. Which is what he would like to do with this woman. Secrete her away somewhere for his own personal enjoyment.

"Karim?"

Dimly, as if from a distance, Hassan heard the melodic sound of her voice, and his eyes dropped to her lips. A sudden tightness encircled his chest as he studied their delectable curve. They looked so soft. Soft and mobile and made to be kissed.

Karim was out of his tiny little mind, Hassan thought as he remembered his brother's description of her. Calling her "kind of attractive" was like calling their father "kind of rich"—the understatement of the year. Kali Whitman was the most sensually alluring woman he had ever seen.

He froze as she unexpectedly leaned toward him and kissed his cheek. His guts clenched painfully at the feel of her lips against his skin, and it was all he could do not to grab her and capture her mouth with his own. He wanted—

His head examined, he thought uneasily. Kali Whitman had been taken advantage of enough by his brother without him compounding the sin by kissing her.

Kali stared up into his face, instinctively shaking her head in an attempt to banish the surge of desire that had so unexpectedly engulfed her when she'd kissed him. What was the matter with her? she wondered uncertainly. She'd kissed Karim when she'd accepted his proposal. Or rather he'd kissed her. A rather restrained touching of their lips that she found vaguely pleasant. So why was it different this time?

And it was different. For a timeless moment she'd completely lost track of what she'd wanted to say to him. All she'd been able to think about was how she'd felt. Excited and full of anticipation. As if he really were a beloved fiancé who'd just returned from an interminable absence.

Troubled, Kali studied his face, looking for a clue to explain her strange reaction. She couldn't find one. Except for appearing slightly paler, as if he'd spent the entire two weeks of his conference in Australia inside, he looked exactly the same as she remembered. Her inexplicable sense of disorientation grew as she suddenly noticed the silvery sparks that seemed to swirl through his night-dark eyes. Funny, she'd never noticed them before. She blinked, and they were gone, making her wonder if she really had seen them.

"Um, I..." Hassan said, and Kali winced at the uncertain note in his voice. Poor Karim, he'd asked her to marry him because she was a levelheaded, intelligent woman not given to romantic excesses, and here she was staring at him like a teenager unexpectedly faced with her favorite rock star.

Feeling gauche, Kali rushed to say, "I can't tell you how glad I am to see you. I was afraid you wouldn't get back in time."

"In time?" Hassan repeated, looking for an opening to break his news.

Kali stepped back. The added distance helped her to think a little more clearly. From here she couldn't smell the delicious scent that clung to him. It reminded her of woodlands and sunshine and crisp autumn air. And it wasn't the one he'd been wearing the night he'd taken her out to celebrate their engagement. Perhaps it was something he'd picked up in Australia? If so, she hoped he'd brought plenty of it back with him because it was—

A distraction, she hurriedly cut off the thought. She needed to concentrate on her problem, not on how she was finding Karim so inexplicably attractive.

"Karim—"

"Hassan," he corrected her.

Kali blinked in confusion, wondering why he'd suddenly decided he wanted to be called by a nickname. Worry about it later, she told herself. For now she needed to focus on a more urgent problem.

"My mother called last night to warn me that my nephew's christening is tomorrow," she said.

"Warn?" Hassan picked up on the odd word. He'd been to a couple of christenings, and he couldn't remember anything about the ceremony that would necessitate a warning.

Kali grimaced. "You remember when I accepted your proposal I said that a marriage based on friendship and shared interests was what I wanted, too?"

Hassan frowned, taken aback. She still thought he was his brother, but why? He'd told her his name was Hassan. Unless Karim hadn't bothered to tell her that he had a twin brother? Or even a brother named Hassan?

He opened his mouth to explain who he really was, but before he could get the words out she continued.

"You see, I didn't mention it at the time, but the reason I feel that way is because I had an experience with the falling-madly-in-love bit. And it was a disaster."

Hassan was appalled at the echo of remembered pain and humiliation he could see shimmering in the depths of her gorgeous eyes. He wanted to thump the lout who was responsible for that look.

"I take it he turned out to be a jerk?"

Kali sighed. "No, it would have been a whole lot easier to deal with if he had been. To make a long, sad story short, a month before the wedding Bart met my younger sister, Annette, for the first time. It was a classic case of love at first sight for them both. Bart married her instead of me."

Driven by a need to console her, Hassan reached out and pulled Kali's slender body against his, holding her comfortingly close.

"That must have been rough," he finally said.

Kali closed her eyes as she savored the feel of his hard body pressing into her much-softer curves. He felt so good. So solidly reassuring, and he was showing far more empathy than her short acquaintance with him would have led her to believe he possessed. A fact that pleased her since it argued well for the success of their marriage.

Stepping out of his arms, she said, "I was pretty upset about Bart's defection at the time, but that was almost two years ago. I've long since gotten over him. In fact, these days I find him a bit of a bore. The problem is that my family thinks I'm harboring this great unrequited love for him. When I try to tell them that I could care less, they just smile and tell me that I'm being so brave."

Hassan chuckled at her indignant expression, and the warm sound rolled through Kali, drowning her annoyance. She'd never heard Hassan chuckle before. It was the most sexually enticing sound she'd ever experienced. And the most distracting. She fought to keep her focus on what she wanted to say and not on how she felt.

"So I thought that if I were to take you with me to the christening of Bart and Annette's baby tomorrow and introduce you to my family, they'll realize that I'm not still hankering after Bart.

"And you did say that we'd go out and meet them when you got back," she added when he didn't respond.

Now what? Hassan wondered in dismay. This was hardly the time to tell her that not only wasn't he Karim, but Karim had changed his mind about marrying her. She'd be humiliated when she had to go home and tell her family that she'd been rejected by yet another fiancé.

Hassan stared down into her soft, brown eyes and felt a surge of tenderness at the uncertainty he could see there. He couldn't do it to her. Not without some warning. And his bad news could easily wait until after the christening. In fact, it would probably be better to tell her then. That way she'd have some time to figure out the best way to tell her family about Karim's defection.

And he did have the weekend free. He didn't have to be back in Boston until Monday morning.

But to impersonate his brother… That was the kind of impulsive behavior that had always characterized Karim, not him. He was the cautious twin. The one who could always be counted on to do the right thing.

But wasn't minimizing the impact Karim's defection had on Kali the right thing to do? Or was he simply rationalizing his inexplicable desire to see more of her even though he knew perfectly well that nothing could ever come of it.

His motives were irrelevant, he finally decided. His family owed Kali a fiancé for the weekend. Since he was the only one in America at the moment, it was up to him to pay the debt.

"I'll go," Hassan blurted out and then winced at the curt sound of his acceptance. He'd sounded as if he were agreeing to something he didn't want to do, and it wasn't like that at all.

"Thanks, Karim. Um... Hassan. Why do you want to be called Hassan all of a sudden?" she asked.

"It's my nickname in the family," he lied. "And I much prefer it to Karim."

"Oh," Kali muttered, wondering why he hadn't mentioned his preference of names when she'd accepted his proposal. Although there hadn't been much opportunity for him to tell her anything so far, she reminded herself. The only time they'd had together was that one rushed evening before he'd had to fly to Australia. This really was the first chance he'd had.

Hassan shifted from one handmade shoe to the other as he quickly sifted through his mind, looking for another topic of conversation. One that didn't have any hidden dangers to it. Not only did the thoughtful expression on her face make him very uneasy, but he didn't want to leave. He didn't want to go back to Karim's empty apartment. He wanted to stay here and listen to the seductive sound of Kali's voice.

He wanted to do a whole lot more than talk to her, he admitted. His eyes instinctively homed in on her luscious lips. He wanted to pull her back into his arms and cover her mouth with his. He wanted to taste the essence of her. He wanted to breathe in the luxuriant floral scent

that clung to her. She was like an erotic gift that a benevolent deity had packaged for some lucky man.

A gift! He suddenly remembered that one took a present to christenings.

"What did you buy for the baby?"

"Nothing yet," Kali said. "I was going to pick something up during my lunch hour yesterday, but like most
Fridays I wound up running late and never got around
to it."

"Why don't we go and buy something now?"

The sudden spurt of pleasure that shot through Kali
at the thought of spending the afternoon with him caught
her by surprise. But why shouldn't she find pleasure in
his company? She was going to marry the man. It was
probably just the thought of spending tomorrow, with
her sister giving her guilty looks, that had unsettled her.
Once the christening was over, things would return to
normal.

"I'd love to. I—" Kali paused as she suddenly remembered something. "Did you bring my boomerang?"

"Boomerang?" he asked cautiously.

"You forgot to get it." She gave him a ruefully ex-
asperated look that made him want to kiss it off her
lips...and then to keep on kissing her until she couldn't
remember the first thing about boomerangs.

"I just forgot to bring it with me," Hassan said, hastily improvising. "I'll give it to you tomorrow."

"Would you mind if I used your bathroom before we
go shopping?" As soon as he asked, he wished he
hadn't. He had no idea where her bathroom was, and his
brother would surely have known.

"Help yourself." Kali made a faint gesture toward the
hallway at the back of the living room.

Hassan walked toward it, trying to look more sure of

himself than he felt. To his relief, the bathroom door was ajar.

Slipping inside, he hastily closed the door behind him. He turned the water on full force to hide the sound of his voice, hurriedly dialed his father's consulate on his cell phone and asked for the consul, Mohammed. A minute later, Hassan had arranged for a boomerang to be delivered the following morning to Karim's apartment.

Deep in thought, Hassan left the bathroom. Now, if he were buying Kali a gift it certainly wouldn't be an oddly shaped piece of wood. It would be something very personal and highly feminine. Something like jewelry. Maybe emeralds to highlight the tawny tints in her hair. Yes, that was it. He'd buy her a necklace with an emerald suspended from a long golden chain. Long enough so that the jewel would rest in the cleft between her breasts. He felt his guts clench as his mind pictured her wearing such a necklace and nothing else.

"Ready to go?" Kali's voice dragged him out of his delightful daydream.

What was the matter with him? he wondered uneasily as he walked toward the front door with Kali. He hadn't fantasized this much about a woman since he'd been an adolescent and his every second thought had been of sex. Now he was a grown man, a highly trained pediatrician, who knew that sex without commitment had no place in his life. And who also knew that he couldn't make a commitment to any Western woman. For her sake.

He tried to ignore the sense of loss that filled him at the thought of never making love to Kali.

"What are we going to buy the child?" Hassan asked, once they were in the elevator.

"Well… I'm not sure. I doubt that Eddie needs anything. My mother started buying things when she found out my sister was pregnant, and she hasn't stopped since.''

"How about the traditional silver porringer?"

"What's a porringer?"

"I think it's a bowl that you put cereal in, but I wouldn't give you odds on it."

She grinned at him. "How can I ask to see something when I'm not even sure what it is?"

"Easy. You simply walk into a jewelry store, stare down the length of your nose at the clerk and demand to see a silver porringer." He mimicked one of his father's imperious looks to demonstrate.

Kali felt a chill sweep through her as her gaze moved up over his clenched jaw and tightly compressed lips, but her sense of apprehension dissolved when she reached his eyes and saw the devilment dancing in their dark depths. It totally dispelled the autocratic expression he was trying to create.

Smiling she reached up and ran her fingertips along his jawline. "No one who looks into your eyes is ever going to buy your impersonation of a despot."

Hassan felt a tiny muscle beneath his left eye twitch at the tantalizing sensation of her fingertips moving over his skin. Instinctively he captured her hand and pressed a kiss to her palm.

Her skin felt warm and infinitely intriguing. His tongue darted out to taste it, and a sense of satisfaction filled him as he saw her eyes widen in reaction. Whatever it was that he felt when he was around her, she obviously felt something, too. Or was it that she was reacting to him because she thought he was Karim? The appalling thought effectively doused his ardor, and he dropped her hand as if burned.

"Are you the baby's godmother?" Hassan clung to

the relatively safe subject of the christening like a life-line.

Kali gulped in air, trying to get enough breath to answer him. She felt as if his kiss had seared her, leaving a permanent imprint of his lips on her skin. Despite the fact that she knew her reaction was highly illogical, it didn't change the way she felt.

Worry about your strange reaction later, she told herself. For now she needed to concentrate on treating him as she always had. As a mildly sexy, highly intelligent, very likable man. Whom she was going to marry. The tantalizing thought did nothing for her already-shaky composure.

"I'm not the godmother," Kali finally answered him. "If you can believe it, my mother told me that Bart feels it would be too painful for me. I swear, sometimes I want to grab Bart by one of his appalling ties and shake him until his sense of overweening importance falls out!"

"Are they?"

Kali blinked in confusion. "What?"

"Are his ties appalling?"

"Yes. Clashing splotches of color, not tastefully modern like—" Her voice faded away when she noticed the somber magnificence of his navy-and-green striped silk tie.

Uh-oh, Hassan thought. He'd completely forgotten Karim's penchant for avant-garde neckwear. "This is my old school tie," he hurriedly offered an explanation, hoping she wouldn't know what the Eton tie really looked like.

Kali nodded, although the thoughtful look in her eyes made him uneasy.

Just how smart was she? he wondered, trying to remember what Karim had said about her. It hadn't been much. Just that she was a psychologist, which meant she was used to looking beneath the surface of things. And if she were to look at him too closely...

It wouldn't matter, he assured himself as he followed her out of the building. His impersonation wouldn't last long enough for her to figure out that he wasn't Karim. By tomorrow evening he'd have told her the truth and... His mind shied away from the thought of what would follow.

"There's a taxi." Kali waved madly to attract its attention, and Hassan determinedly banished his worries.

"Where to?" the driver demanded, when they were in the taxi.

"Blackwells over by Times Square." Hassan gave him the name of his mother's favorite jewelry store. "If anyone in New York City has a porringer it'll be Blackwells," Hassan told Kali.

When they reached the jeweler's, Kali climbed out of the cab and examined the display windows while Hassan paid the fare. The elaborate ruby-and-diamond necklace casually draped across a piece of black velvet gave her doubts about the wisdom of going inside. That necklace looked as if it had come from the Hermitage's collection of the Russian royal family's jewelry.

"Hassan," she said when he joined her, "I don't know what the Institute pays you, but I get the impression I don't make enough to shop in this place." She glanced down again at the beautiful necklace. "In fact, I could get an inferiority complex just window shopping here."

Hassan studied her uncertainly, wondering if she were serious. She seemed like such a self-possessed woman.

So sure of herself and her place in the world that it was hard for him to believe she could suffer from some of the same social insecurities that he did.

He frowned as he suddenly realized the full implication of her words. She thought Karim was dependent on what he earned as a research scientist. Obviously Karim hadn't told her that their father ruled a very oil-rich country in the Middle East. So rich that Saad Dev'a's citizens enjoyed one of the highest standards of living in the world.

Why hadn't Karim told her? Hassan wondered. Because he hadn't wanted Kali's decision to marry him to be based on his wealth? Or had he been afraid that Kali might turn him down if she realized just how different their backgrounds were?

Hassan didn't know, but he did know that Karim knew women far better than he could ever hope to. If Karim hadn't wanted Kali to know his financial worth, then he'd keep it a secret, too.

"I have a thrifty nature," he finally said. "So that when I do want to splurge a little, I can afford to."

"But I can't let you pay for Eddie's gift."

"Oh, yes, you can. We're engaged, remember."

"Yes, but—"

"But nothing," Hassan pulled open the door. "Come on."

Reluctantly Kali followed Hassan into the elegant store.

"Good afternoon." The middle-aged clerk gave Kali a practiced smile before his gaze moved to Hassan. He instantly priced the hand-tailored perfection of Hassan's suit, and his smile widened. "Sir. How may I be of service to you this afternoon?"

"We would like to see a christening gift," Hassan said.

"Certainly. If you and," the clerk's eyes dropped to Kali's ringless fingers, "the lady will sit down, I will be glad to show you some appropriate gifts. Or did you already have something in mind?"

Hassan waited until Kali sat in one of the chairs the clerk had pointed to before he sat down beside her.

"We want a silver porringer," Hassan said.

"Ah! A traditionalist after my own heart." The clerk beamed at him. "Just a moment while I check our stock. I'll be right back."

Kali watched the man disappear into the back and then whispered, "I don't believe it. He really does have a porringer."

True to his word, the man was back almost immediately carrying a black lacquered tray holding three dark blue velvet bags. "We have several porringers in stock. These—" he pulled two of them out of their protective bags and set them on the counter in front of Kali "—are strictly traditional.

"This one," he pointed to the fairly plain one, "is a copy of one that George IV of England gave to the Marquis of Londonderry at his christening in 1821. While this one—" He held up an ornately cast one "—is a copy of one from an earlier period. As you can see, it has a more baroque feel to it."

"They're beautiful," Kali said, wondering if the unknown Marquis had really eaten his cereal out of anything that valuable.

"Nice, but we wanted something a little more ostentatious," Hassan said, and Kali suppressed a groan. Much more ostentatious and between them they wouldn't be able to pay for it.

The clerk unexpectedly grinned, looking far more human. "In that case, I have exactly the thing for you. It was a special order that was unfortunately canceled. It is most definitely impressive."

He picked up the last velvet sack and pulled out a small gold bowl which he set reverently in front of Kali. "As you can see from the luster, it is almost pure gold. Which of course means that it is nowhere near as sturdy as the silver ones. It is meant strictly for display."

"It's beautiful," Kali breathed, "but far too impractical," she hurriedly added at Hassan's speculative expression.

"We'll take it," Hassan said, ignoring Kali's indrawn hiss. He was determined she was going to have a gift to take that would impress the hell out of her ex-fiancé.

And a ring. Hassan remembered how the clerk had automatically checked Kali's hand for an engagement ring. Bart would be bound to do the same thing.

"While we're here, would you show us some engagement rings?" Hassan said.

"Certainly, sir." The man rubbed his hands together, and Kali could almost see him mentally calculating his commission. "Does the lady have a choice of stone?"

Does the lady have a choice at all, Kali thought with an uncertain look at Hassan. What was he up to? When she'd accepted his proposal, he'd asked her if she'd wanted a ring, and she'd said no, seeing no reason for him to go to the expense for what was to be merely a merger of friends. He'd agreed with her then, so why had he changed his mind now?

"An emerald," Hassan said, remembering his earlier fantasy.

"An excellent choice with the lady's coloring," the

man approved. "We have several fine stones in stock at
the moment. I'll just get them out of the safe."

He hurried toward the back of the store, almost as if
he were afraid they might change their minds and leave
before he could clinch a sale.

Kali barely waited until the man was out of hearing
before she turned to Hassan. "We decided against a
ring."

"You need one for tomorrow," Hassan insisted.
"Your family isn't going to believe that you're really
engaged if you don't have a ring. Bart gave you one
when you got engaged, didn't he?"

"Yes, a diamond." Kali's eyes automatically dropped
to her left hand, remembering the ring he'd given her.
It had been small, but she'd loved it out of all proportion
to its size, seeing it as confirmation of Bart's love.

"You don't still have it, do you?" Hassan asked,
shocked at the anger filling him at her faraway expression. He was angry on her behalf, he assured himself.
Angry that she had been so badly used. It didn't matter
to him personally. It couldn't. He'd only known her a
few hours.

"Certainly not. I gave it back to him. I have no idea
what happened to it."

The clerk emerged from the back room and set a small
tray of rings down in front of them with a flourish.

Kali looked down at them, trying to keep her appreciation of their beauty out of her face. They looked
frightfully expensive. But maybe Hassan was looking on
the ring as an investment? That was probably it, she
decided, feeling fractionally better. While she preferred
to invest in stocks and bonds, she knew lots of people
bought gold and precious gems as a hedge against infla-
tion.

"What about this one?" Hassan picked up a large, square-cut stone set in yellow gold and handed it to her.

Obediently Kali tried it on, her eyes widening in appreciation at the way the magnificent gem caught the light.

"Do you like it?" Hassan asked.

"It is the most beautiful ring I've ever seen," she said, instinctively blurting out the truth.

"We'll take it," Hassan said in satisfaction. He'd been right. Emeralds were the perfect choice for Kali.

"Um, Hassan." Kali shot him a warning look. Investment or not, they ought to at least ask how much it was before they committed themselves.

"It's too loose." She grabbed the first excuse she could think of.

"No problem at all," the clerk said cheerfully. "I can have it resized within the hour."

What's going to be resized is both our bank accounts, Kali thought, but somehow she just couldn't refuse to accept it. Not with Hassan looking so pleased with himself. But why was he so pleased with himself? She had absolutely no idea, and that bothered her. She'd thought she had a pretty good understanding of both his personality and what motivated him.

But his insistence on buying her a ring seemed completely out of character for him...or else she'd misread his character in the first place. She didn't find either possibility reassuring.

Uneasily she watched as Hassan followed the clerk over to the counter to pay for their purchases. What other surprises did Hassan have in store for her? The idea both worried and exhilarated her.

Two

Hassan shifted the brightly painted boomerang from his right hand to his left, patted his suit jacket pocket to make sure Kali's ring was still there and then rapped sharply on her apartment door. Giving her that ring had become very important to him. He wanted her to have a memento of him that had nothing to do with his brother. And tonight, after he told her the truth, he'd insist she keep it.

Kali flung the door open. "You're early."

"Traffic was light," he improvised, suddenly remembering that Karim was perpetually late to everything.

"Come in." Kali stepped back, when what she wanted to do was put her arms around him and kiss him. To breathe in the cold tang of the outdoors that he brought with him and then to snuggle even closer to savor the scent of his new cologne. A compulsion she was at a total loss to explain. It made no sense that a two-week absence should have intensified her previously tepid sexual curiosity about him to the point where it was in imminent danger of becoming an obsession.

One thing was certain, she thought as she surreptitiously studied him, her newfound fascination was not reciprocated or he would have kissed her when he'd arrived. But maybe he was waiting for a sign from her that she would welcome a kiss? But what if he wasn't and she gave him a sign. What would he think then?

"Here's your boomerang." Hassan handed it to her, giving her hopelessly tangled thoughts a safer direction.

"Thank you. I always wanted a real Australian boomerang. The ones I had as a kid never worked, and I always wondered if it was because I simply didn't have the knack for throwing them or if it was because they weren't authentic.

"What are all these figures painted on it?" she asked.

"Aborigine pictographs," Hassan quoted what Mohammed had told him. "They're supposed to make game susceptible to it."

"I see." Kali glanced speculatively around the living room. If she didn't throw it very hard, there was just room enough to see if there was any curve in its trajectory.

"You can't throw that inside." Hassan correctly interpreted her look.

She gave him an impish grin that inexplicably made him feel ten years old again. But not quite, he realized. Now the feeling had sexual overtones that he hadn't even been aware had existed at that age.

"Of course I can," Kali said. "Whether I should or not is entirely another matter."

He was about to point out the danger of shattering a window on the sixth floor when he remembered that he was supposed to be Karim. His twin certainly would see nothing wrong with playing with a boomerang indoors. In fact, Karim would probably be demanding the first turn.

"I'm not going to throw it hard," Kali explained as she tested the boomerang's balance on her fingertips. "I just want to see if it curves."

To Hassan's relief, she turned toward the kitchen, away from the windows, and gave it a restrained toss. It flew ten feet straight ahead before dropping like a stone.

"I don't think boomerangs ever work!" Kali complained "I'll bet it's all just a lie put out by the Australian Tourist Board to sell the blasted things."

"Maybe you simply haven't said the proper incantations."

"Incantations?" Kali looked up, her attention caught by the odd note in his voice. "What kind of incantations?"

"Boomerangs are hunting weapons and as such exclusively the property of men. You're a woman."

And what a woman, he thought, allowing his gaze to linger on the swell of her breasts beneath her cream silk blouse.

"Maybe what I need is some woman magic to counter the masculine pictographs," she said, trying to keep the conversation lighthearted, so that if he withdrew from her it wouldn't embarrass either of them. And if he didn't withdraw...

She took a deep breath. She might be able to finagle a kiss out of this.

"Woman magic?" Hassan asked.

"Uh-huh, woman magic is a very potent force in all primitive societies." Kali slowly ran the tip of her tongue over her dry lips as she scrambled for a way to move things out of the realm of spoken language and into that of body language.

Her confidence level soared when she noticed his eyes following her tongue's movement.

Slowly Kali advanced toward him, drawing pictures in the air with her fingers as she came.

"I am woman. I am all-powerful." She sing-songed the words, not stopping until she was almost touching him.

To her surprise and delight, Hassan suddenly reached out and pulled her up against him. She landed against his hard chest with a bump that momentarily dislodged rational thought. Automatically she put out her hands to steady herself, grasping his arms. She could feel his hard biceps through the sleek wool material of his gray suit. It was an intriguing combination. Much like Hassan himself was turning out to be.

"Women are many things, but powerful isn't one of them." Hassan couldn't seem to drag his gaze away from her lips. She had the most alluring mouth he'd ever seen.

"You mean this isn't the time to tell you that I was the best student in my self-defense class at the Y?" Kali tilted her head back, and the movement pushed her breasts into his chest, sending a wave of desire spiraling through her.

"Really?" Hassan's arms tightened, lifting her off her feet and holding her securely against him. "Try to get free."

Now why would she want to do a dumb thing like that? Kali wondered, when he felt like the embodiment of every sexual fantasy she'd ever had as well as a few she hadn't gotten around to yet.

"But it's woman magic I control," she murmured,

nuzzling her face against his neck. "And woman magic is a little different from brute strength. For example," she trailed her lips along his jawline and began to nuzzle the skin behind his ear. She could feel his body's instant response, and it fed her self-confidence.

She took a deep, indulgent breath of the delicious aroma that clung to him, allowing it to fill her lungs. Savoring the sensations unfurling in her, Kali licked the spot she'd been caressing, smiling happily when he gasped.

Emboldened she traced back over his jawline with her lips, exploring the exact texture of his skin. It had a faintly raspy feel to it as if he had a very heavy beard.

Her speculation was cut short as Hassan suddenly turned his head and captured her mouth with his. His lips pressed forcefully against hers, demanding that she open her mouth to his exploration. Instinctively she obeyed, and he shoved his tongue inside with a rough hunger Kali found incredibly sexy.

Reaction poured over her in waves, raising goose bumps on her flesh. Her arms tightened around his shoulders, trying to bind him closer. She hadn't realized that a simple kiss could feel like this. She could even hear bells.

A monumental sense of loss filled her as Hassan suddenly dropped his arms and stepped back.

Kali gulped in air, struggling to get control of her turbulent emotions. It wasn't easy. She felt shaken to the very core of her being. Totally unlike herself. And totally unlike the sensible, competent woman Hassan had proposed to. The fear that he might notice her unprecedented reaction and wonder about it was like a shower of cold water on her overheated emotions.

Kali ran her fingers down over the smooth line of her green tweed skirt willing them to stop trembling.

"Here, I almost forgot," Hassan said.

Kali looked up to find him holding out the engagement ring he'd bought her yesterday.

Kali stared down at the exquisite thing, wondering how anyone could ever forget something so beautiful...even for a moment. The huge emerald seemed to glow as if lit from within.

"It's even more gorgeous than I remember," she said, uncertain as to whether she should put it on or let him, as a couple would do in a normal engagement.

But she didn't want a normal engagement. She'd already tried falling in love, and it had been a complete disaster. Her cool, considered arrangement with Hassan was much better.

She looked up into Hassan's dark eyes, and her heart skipped a beat. At least it *had* been cool and considered, she amended. But for some reason, ever since Hassan had gotten back from Australia, he'd been different.

No, she corrected herself as she studied his familiar features. Hassan wasn't different. What was different was how she was reacting to him. And she had no idea why.

Hassan answered her unspoken question by taking her hand and slipping the ring on her finger.

"A perfect fit," Hassan announced, wanting to kiss her again. He wanted to see if it felt the same or if his explosive reaction to their earlier kiss had been a fluke. He wanted...some common sense. He choked off his desire with monumental effort. He had absolutely no business kissing her, because tonight he was going to tell her the truth.

But until then he was playing the part of her fiancé

and if he didn't play the part convincingly, he wouldn't
fool her family. And this whole exercise would have
been a waste.

Kali watched the emotions flitting across his face,
wondering what he was thinking. She didn't have a clue.
Hassan was turning out to be a lot more complicated
than she'd originally thought.

But this wasn't the time to worry about it, she told
herself as the cuckoo clock she'd lugged home from
Germany four years ago suddenly chimed the half hour.

Hurriedly she got her tan dress coat out of the closet
and shrugged into it.

"I told Mom I'd call her from the train station when
we get in," Kali told Hassan as she carefully locked her
apartment door behind them. "Someone will collect
us."

"I've got a car."

"But you hate to drive." She frowned uncertainly at
him.

Damn! Hassan mentally cursed his slip. How could
he have forgotten the car accident that had killed his
uncle and led to the breakup of his parents' happy marriage? Six-year-old Karim had been severely injured.
The whole family had spent the next fifteen years cater-
ing to his every whim. The accident had also left Karim
with a horror of driving. But maybe Karim hadn't told
Kali the reason he didn't drive. He didn't seem to have
told her anything else about his background.

"I wouldn't exactly say that I hate to drive," Hassan
carefully felt his way. "It's more that I find it a nuisance
in New York City. But I thought that it would be better
not to be tied to the Long Island Railroad's schedule.
Especially on a Sunday. So I borrowed a car from a
friend at the consulate."

Kali chuckled. "You sound like you're anticipating a quick getaway. Not that I blame you. The best of families can be pretty heavy going at times."

"I'll say!"

Kali blinked at his heartfelt tone, wondering what he was thinking of. His own family? She frowned when she realized that she knew almost nothing about them. Just a couple of chance comments that added up to the fact that his mother was English and his parents were divorced.

"Hassan, do you have any brothers and sisters?"

"No sisters, but two brothers. I'm parked right out in front of your building." He deliberately changed the subject, hoping he hadn't sounded as abrupt to her as he did to himself. He could hardly give her any specifics about his brothers without lying, and he didn't want to tell any more lies than he absolutely had to.

He held the lobby door open for her and then led her over to the large black Mercedes that Mohammed had loaned him.

"Very impressive." Kali studied the leather interior as Hassan started the car. "I don't think I've ever driven in anything this luxurious before."

"Hmm" Hassan murmured, his mind completely taken up with the sound of her voice. She had the most intriguing voice he'd ever heard in a woman. Low and husky, full of feminine promise. And that was just in a normal, everyday setting. What would her voice sound like if he were to make love to her? Soft and dreamy? A sudden shaft of desire pierced his composure, making him grip the steering wheel tightly. Not now, he thought, forcing himself to concentrate on driving. There were enough distractions on the road without his adding the most dangerous one of all—sexual desire.

* * *

The trip out to Long Island took almost an hour. An hour during which Kali had become increasingly aware of Hassan's physical presence: the way his long fingers competently gripped the wheel; the way his broad shoulders shifted as he steered the car; the length of his long legs so near to her own.

By the time they reached her home, she was beginning to feel rattled. As if she were a music box which had been wound too tightly and now couldn't quite perform the way it was supposed to. But why? The question nagged at her. Why was she responding so strongly to him now, when she never had before?

Could it be because he was being more open with her than he had in the past? Like sharing his family nickname and taking her shopping? But it couldn't be just that. She remembered the unprecedented surge of desire she'd felt when she'd opened the door yesterday afternoon and had seen him standing there. She'd experienced the attraction before he'd even said a word.

Maybe she shouldn't try to figure it out, she considered. Maybe she should simply accept it as a good thing that she was so sexually attracted to the man she was going to marry.

But was it a good thing? she wondered uneasily.

She stole a quick glance at Hassan as he pulled into her parents' driveway. Would Hassan think so? He'd been crystal clear about only wanting a wife who liked him. A wife who wouldn't interfere with his work or make emotional demands on him. What would he say if she were to suddenly tell him that she was fast becoming obsessed with his body?

She sighed. Put like that, it sounded so…juvenile. Adult women of thirty who had agreed to what was essentially a marriage of convenience should be able to control their sexual desires. So why couldn't she?

"Don't worry." Hassan misunderstood the reason for her sigh. "I'll protect you from Bart."

An image of Bart's slightly overweight, definitely out-of-condition body flitted through her mind. Bart wouldn't stand a chance against Hassan. Not that she needed protecting from Bart or anyone else for that matter. She was a modern woman who was the graduate of a self-defense class. She could protect herself.

"Come on. Let's get this show on the road." Kali determinedly shoved open the car door, hoping that Annette and Bart hadn't arrived yet. It would be easier if she could introduce Hassan to her parents first.

Fate turned a deaf ear to her hopes. The first person she saw when she opened the front door was Bart.

"Kali, glad you could make it," he said, sounding to Kali's critical ears just a shade too expansive.

"Bart." Kali nodded. "I'd like you to meet my fiancé, Hassan Rashid."

"Glad to meet you," Bart shook the hand Hassan held out. "I guess you and I have something in common. Or didn't Kali tell you about us?" Bart gave her a conspiratorial look that made Kali want to smack him. Hard. Why did he persist in referring to the past?

"You mean your engagement?" Hassan gave Bart his best imitation of what he and Karim had always called their father's long-suffering-aristocrat-faced-with-erring-peasant expression. "That's what youth is for—to make mistakes. After all, if Kali hadn't experimented when she was young, how would she ever have realized what she really wanted in a man?"

Kali wanted to fling her arms around Hassan and hug him. With just a few words he'd relegated her engagement to Bart to the ranks of a youthful mistake and not a very important one at that.

"I'll let your mother know you're here, Kali." Bart gave Hassan a sour look and escaped into the kitchen.

"You've got to show me how to do that," Kali said.

"Do what?"

"That look you gave Bart. It was inspired. Where did you learn it?"

Hassan chuckled, finding her humor infectious. "From my father. He always used it on—" he hurriedly caught himself before he said Karim and substituted "—me, whenever I'd done something that particularly annoyed him."

"Oh?" Kali felt a momentary flash of unease at the realization that she knew absolutely nothing about his father. What was he like? Would he dislike her? Did he even know that Hassan had proposed to her?

"Hassan," she said slowly, "what is your father going to say about you marrying an American woman?"

"He'll love you," Hassan said, knowing his father would have given his blessing to Karim's marrying her because he intended to live and work in America.

Hassan also knew his father would be violently opposed to him marrying Kali because he was committed to returning to the Middle East once his course in hospital management was completed.

When his uncle's death in the automobile accident had forced his father's return to the kingdom, his parents' marriage had faltered and eventually crumbled. His mother had been unable to adjust to life there. His father certainly wouldn't want that pain revisited on one of his sons.

And he was absolutely right, Hassan admitted. Western women did not belong in the narrow restrictive world of his country.

"Darling, you're here!" Mrs. Whitman rushed into the living room, forestalling any more questions on Kali's part for which Hassan was grateful.

"And you must be Karim." Mrs. Whitman beamed at him. "My goodness, you're tall. For an Arab, I mean."

"Mom, his family calls him Hassan. Hassan, this tactful soul is my mother and— Where's dad?" Kali looked behind her mother.

Mrs. Whitman grimaced. "One of his patients went into labor, and he had to leave. And, what's worse, since it's her first, he has no idea how long it'll be. So annoying when he was looking forward to meeting your fiancé." She smiled at Hassan.

"And I was looking forward to meeting him, Mrs. Whitman," Hassan said cautiously. It sounded as if Kali's father was an obstetrician, but he couldn't be sure. Nor could he ask, because he didn't know if Kali had already told Karim. Which meant his best bet would be to stick to social platitudes, he decided.

"Oh, call me Mom," Mrs. Whitman said. "After all, you'll soon be one of the family. I mean, it's not like last time when…um… Do come in and meet Kali's sister," Mrs. Whitman said hurriedly.

"Mom is not known for thinking before she speaks," Kali whispered to Hassan as they followed her mother into the family room. "But she means well."

As he did with this impersonation, Hassan thought, having a great deal of empathy for Mrs. Whitman.

"Kali, I'm so glad you could make it." Annette looked up from the couch where she was giving her son a bottle of juice.

"We wouldn't have missed it for the world." Kali put her arm through Hassan's and drew him close to her, almost losing her train of thought when she felt the hard length of him pressing against her side.

"Annette, this is Hassan Rashid, my fiancé." Some of the excitement she was feeling colored her voice, giving it a sensual quality that sent a shiver of awareness through Hassan.

Responding to it, he put his arm around her shoulders and pulled her even closer. She fit perfectly against his side. As if she'd been created expressly for him, he thought fancifully.

"I'm glad to meet you, Hassan." Annette didn't sound any too sure of the fact.

"And I you," Hassan said. "I owe you a debt of gratitude."

Annette blinked uncertainly. "Me?"

"Yes, if you hadn't married her first fiancé, I would have missed the love of my life." Hassan said smoothly.

"You're welcome. Don't you think Eddie has grown, Kali?" Annette seemed eager to change the subject.

"Definitely. He's starting to look more like a person and less like a baby."

Eddie reacted to her pronouncement by bursting into tears.

"Here, Hassan, you can hold him." Bart plucked his howling son out of Annette's arms and handed the baby to Hassan. "It'll give you a chance to practice."

To Kali's surprise, Hassan not only took Eddie, but he also competently cradled him against his shoulder as if holding screaming children were something he did every day.

"Hey there, sport, what's wrong?" Hassan gently rubbed the baby's back.

Eddie let out a tremendous belch, hiccuped once and then snuggled his small head against Hassan's broad shoulder.

Kali felt her heart contract at the sight of the large man and the tiny baby. Someday that would be their child Hassan would be holding. A baby that they had made together. The very thought made her feel light-headed.

"You're very good with children, Hassan," Mrs. Whitman said. "Do you have any yourself?"

"No, I've never been married," Hassan replied.

"Marriage isn't what makes babies," Bart chortled.

"Here, let me take him before he dribbles all over that nice suit of yours, Hassan." Annette hurriedly took her son. "Kali, I think he needs changing. Want to come and help me?"

"Yes, dear. Go help your sister," Mrs. Whitman urged. "Bart and I will entertain Hassan for you."

Entertain didn't describe Bart's conversation so far, Kali thought as she reluctantly followed Annette. She had definite misgivings about leaving Hassan in Bart's company. For some reason, Bart had taken a dislike to Hassan the moment he'd set eyes on him.

Kali stifled a sigh. It promised to be a long day. Especially without her father there to keep the conversation on an even keel.

"What time is the ceremony?" Kali asked.

"About three. Everyone else will meet us at the church. We're having the reception in the church basement so Mom doesn't have to clean up the mess."

Annette put the baby down on the changing table and picked up a clean diaper.

When she was finished, she turned to Kali and said, "Kali, are you sure about…"

Annette gestured toward the door.

"Yes," Kali said, rather surprised at the vehemence with which the word came out. But it was true. She really was sure. The doubts that had sprung up while Hassan had been in Australia had completely vanished now that he was back home. She was not only sure that she was doing the right thing by marrying him, she also could hardly wait.

"Oh, I know he's handsome…"

"Very handsome," Kali amended. "He's also sexy as hell."

"That is obvious. He reminds me of that book we read when we were young. You remember the one about the sheik who kidnaps the English girl and winds up marrying her."

"Sorry to deflate your fantasy, but Hassan is most definitely a man of the twentieth century," Kali said, ignoring her earlier doubts.

"But he's foreign."

"So am I, from his perspective."

"Yes, but…"

"But what?"

"Well, Bart thinks that Hassan is just marrying you to get his green card."

Annette was wrong. Bart didn't think! Kali held on to her temper with a real effort. Mainly because she knew that Annette loved her and really did worry about her. About Bart's motives Kali wasn't so sure.

"Annette, Hassan has been in this country since graduate school. He certainly doesn't need marriage to me to give him any legal standing. Now how about letting me hold my favorite nephew."

Annette giggled. "He's your only nephew. Are you and Hassan going to have any kids?"

"Scads," Kali said blithely.

"Kali!" Annette's eyes widened as Kali settled the baby against her shoulder and Annette caught a glimpse of her engagement ring. "Your ring! Let me see it."

Kali switched Eddie to her other shoulder and obligingly held out her left hand.

"My God!" Annette breathed. "It's fantastic. Has Mom seen it?"

"No."

"Then let's show her. Come on," she said, and Kali obediently trailed along behind her, happy to show off her gorgeous ring.

"Mom, look at Kali's engagement ring," Annette said when they returned to the family room. "I've never seen anything so beautiful in my life."

"Let me see, honey." Mrs. Whitman grabbed Kali's hand and held it up. The emerald caught the sunlight pouring in through the patio door and became a blaze of color.

"I've never seen an emerald that big, Hassan," Mrs. Whitman said. "Wherever did you find it?"

"Blackwells," Hassan said.

"Which reminds me, Annette," Kali hurriedly changed the subject before her forthright mother could ask him how much it had cost. "Eddie's christening gift is in my purse. Why don't you get it."

"You didn't have to bring him a gift," Annette said as she delved into Kali's purse and pulled out the gaily wrapped package. "I mean, it's not like you're his godmother. Not that I didn't wanted you to be, but Bart thought…" Annette ground to an embarrassed halt.

"No matter. He's still my nephew," Kali said. "Open your gift."

Annette obediently ripped off the wrapping paper,

gasping when she saw the golden gleam of the bowl. "It's beautiful. Absolutely exquisite."

"But what is it?" Bart asked.

"It's a porringer," Mrs. Whitman spoke up. "I remember my great-grandmother had one from when her mother was christened back in the old country. I didn't even realize they still made them. Let alone in gold."

Kali chuckled. "Neither did I. It was Hassan's suggestion."

"Thank you, Hassan." Annette gave him a wide smile. "It's the nicest gift I've gotten. It makes me feel like I'm part of a long tradition. You're going to be a very nice addition to the family."

No, Kali mentally corrected her sister. Hassan wasn't a nice addition to the family. He was the perfect addition.

Three

"Can I help you with anything, Mom?" Kali asked when the timer sounded in the kitchen and Mrs. Whitman jumped to her feet as if eager to escape the stilted conversation in the family room.

As was Kali herself. If she had to listen to any more of Bart's cracks about foreigners who were flooding America and grabbing up all the good jobs, she'd forget the necessity of maintaining peace and say something very rude. The wonder was that Hassan hadn't already done so. He'd never been one to suffer fools gladly, and yet he hadn't retaliated once to Bart's barbs.

Perhaps he was swallowing his anger for her sake just as she was doing for her sister's sake, Kali decided. Hassan did have beautiful manners.

"No, dear. I have lunch under control. Although you could run down to the basement and bring me up some

of those brandied peaches I put up last summer and
maybe a jar of dilled green beans, too."

"Sure. Come help me, Hassan," Kali said, wanting
to give him a respite from Bart.

"You need help to carry two jars up from the basement, Kali?" Bart sniped.

Annette unexpectedly giggled. "Oh, darling, don't be
dense. Remember what it was like when we were engaged."

Kali ignored both of them.

"I wouldn't blame you for canceling the engagement
after today," Kali told Hassan once they were safely in
the basement. "I can't figure out what on earth is the
matter with Bart. I mean I've known he was a bore for
years now, but he's always been a reasonably good-
mannered bore. Today he's acting like—"

"Like he's suffering from a terminal case of jealousy," Hassan said.

Kali turned from the shelves she'd been perusing and
looked back at Hassan. He appeared enormous in the
low-ceilinged basement.

"Of me? But why? It was my sister he wanted to
marry. There hasn't been anything between us since he
first saw her almost two years ago."

"But during that time he's gotten into the habit of
thinking of you as being in love with him. It strokes his
ego to think that you're pining for him."

"And my bringing you home has pretty effectively
shattered his self-delusion, because there is no way anyone could compare the pair of you and think that I was
still hankering after Bart." Kali followed Hassan's logic
a step further.

Hassan felt a quick surge of pleasure at her words that
just as quickly faded. It didn't matter what she thought

of him since nothing could come from their brief relationship.

Kali turned and began to check the shelves for the jars her mother wanted.

Fascinated, he watched the slight movement of her hips beneath her slim skirt as she moved jars around the shelf. She had the most fantastic figure. Softly feminine and gently rounded, hinting at all kinds of delights.

His breath caught as she twisted slightly, trying to reach something in the back, and he caught a glimpse of the shape of her breast beneath her cream silk blouse. What would her breasts look like? he wondered. Would they be as soft as her face? Or would they be softer? Would...

"Here. Hold this while I try and find those peaches she wants." Kali handed him a jar of green beans and then dragged an aluminum stepladder in front of the shelves.

Climbing to the top step, Kali began to absently move jars, her mind still taken up with what Hassan had said about Bart. It wasn't that she thought he was wrong, because she didn't. Once he'd pointed it out, it was obvious. What bothered her was that Hassan had seen it in the first place. In all the time she'd known him, he'd never shown the slightest tendency to look beneath the surface of a situation. In fact, his sometimes maddening tendency to simply accept things at face value had been one of the negatives she'd considered when she'd weighed the pros and cons of marrying him. And yet, he'd read the situation with Bart far more accurately than she had, and she was a trained psychologist.

So why hadn't he ever shown that skill before? Kali stared blankly at a jar of minted pears. Never once during any of the neurological tests he'd performed on her patients had he shown the slightest insight into the kids' actions.

Could it be because Bart was an adult and her patients had been kids?

Kali suddenly let out a horrified squeak and jerked backward when a huge, black spider ran across her hand. She teetered on the edge of the stepladder for a second, fighting for balance and then tipped over to land against Hassan's chest.

His left arm closed around her rib cage, holding her crushed up against him, and she instinctively clutched his neck holding on for dear life.

"Why are you taking dives off stepladders?" He sounded no more than mildly curious.

"There was a spider, and I touched it! A huge spider!" Kali shuddered at the appalling memory of hairy legs running over her skin.

"Did you hurt it?"

"It! To hell with *it!* I've been traumatized. Feel my heartbeat." She tightened her grip around his neck, pressing herself against his chest. The heat from his body seeped into her breasts making them tingle with reaction. He felt so fantastic. So quintessentially masculine. So everything she wanted in a man.

"I can't quite make it out." Hassan's voice sounded slightly strained to her.

Encouraged, she tightened her stranglehold on him. "Is that better?" she murmured.

"Just a minute." He stretched slightly and deposited the jar he'd been holding on the shelf behind her. Then he shifted her weight slightly, molding her pliant body more closely to him.

"I still can't count your heartbeat," he finally said.

Kali shivered slightly as his warm breath wafted across her cheek causing the skin to tighten.

"But having been a Boy Scout in my youth, I have an alternate plan."

"How nice," Kali muttered, too busy enjoying the sensation of being squashed up against him to pay much attention to what he was saying.

Pressing his lips against her neck, he nuzzled the tiny pulse throbbing near the base. Kali's heart began to race at the intoxicating sensations that tore through her.

"That's better," he said, "now I can feel the blood pounding through your carotid artery. You're definitely—"

"Hey, what's taking you two so long down there?" Bart's querulous voice floated down the stairs.

Kali gritted her teeth in annoyance. She raised her head to yell at Bart and immediately forgot all about him when she found her mouth only centimeters from Hassan's. Unable to resist the temptation, she placed a quick kiss on his seductive lips.

"Hey, Mom needs her stuff," Bart persisted.

"And you need to grow up," Kali called up at him.

"Well, excuse me for trying to help Mom!" Bart yelled back.

"I'd like to excuse him period," Kali grumbled as she stepped out of Hassan's arms. "For the rest of the day, in fact."

Climbing back up the stepladder, she gingerly continued her search for the peaches. She could hardly wait for the day to be over, so she could go home and hopefully get Hassan by himself for a few minutes.

Although, maybe that wasn't such a good idea, she considered. Hassan had been very specific that theirs was to be a marriage of friends, and if she were to start making sexual demands on him, he might begin to think that she was trying to change the original premise of their marriage.

He might even think that she had fallen in love with him! And she hadn't, she assured herself. She might have discovered a hitherto unsuspected sexual fascination with him, but that certainly didn't mean that she was in love with the man.

Sexual curiosity was perfectly normal, she assured herself. Especially about the man she was going to marry. At least, in her culture it was normal. But what about in Hassan's culture?

Kali felt a tiny frisson of unease skitter through her. Despite the fact that she tended to forget it, he wasn't American or even Western. Just how much of the traditional Middle-Eastern attitude toward women did Hassan subconsciously subscribe to?

The tiny, niggling doubts about his background that had shadowed her since the moment she'd accepted his proposal suddenly flared up.

Blindly she shoved aside a jar of sweet cherries. Surely if he harbored extremely restrictive views toward women and their place in society he'd have given her some clues to the fact long before now.

Although, he hadn't told her something as basic as his family's nickname for him until yesterday, she remembered. The thought increased her sense of unease. What other surprises might he be concealing?

They were only engaged, she reminded herself, trying to soothe her fears. They hadn't even discussed a wedding date yet. She had plenty of time to get to know him better.

Finally she located what seemed to be the last jar of

brandied peaches and, climbing down, put the stepladder away.

"Did that spider really frighten you?" Hassan eyed her worried features uncertainly.

"I hate spiders," she grabbed at the excuse he was offering. "Come on. Let's give these to Mom."

They might as well, Hassan thought as he followed her up the stairs. That fool Bart had irrevocably destroyed her lighthearted mood.

Not that he should have been kissing her, anyway, he reminded himself. After tonight he'd never see her again. He swallowed against the unexpected sense of loss that filled him.

Contrary to Kali's fears, the day did eventually end and they were able to leave. A fact she was sure Hassan must be equally grateful for. Usually he was the life and soul of the party, but today he'd been distinctly subdued. Not that she blamed him. Bart's seemingly endless supply of snide cracks would have been enough to chill the most ebullient of spirits.

"Thanks for being such a good sport about today," she said, once they were safely on the road back to New York City.

"Actually I found the experience rather interesting. What I can't understand is what you ever saw in Bart."

Kali shrugged. "I met him when we were both volunteers at a weekend retreat our church was holding for teens. I really liked the way he put himself out to help. And he can be very good company when he wants to be.

"Anyway, we started dating. There wasn't any big thing to put me off him. Just the odd comment, which would give me pause. Such as what he thought a wife's role in a marriage should be. But since he was reasonable about lots of things, I thought that we could work out some kind of compromise, such as me working part time when our children were small. When Bart flatly refused to even consider the idea, I started to reexamine our whole relationship and what was really important to me. But before I could come to any kind of conclusion about what I wanted to do, he met my sister and the decision was made for me.''

''He...'' Hassan suddenly swerved to the right, skillfully holding the car on the very edge of the road's gravel shoulder as a pickup truck accelerated around them, passing on the double yellow line, and almost hitting the van in the oncoming lane.

''The fool!'' Kali swallowed, trying to force her heart back down her throat. ''What's he trying to do?''

''Commit suicide and take as many people with him as he can. Get the cell phone out of the glove compartment and call the state police. Maybe they'll be able to intercept him before—''

Hassan was interrupted by the squeal of brakes, followed almost immediately by the sound of a tremendous crunch.

''Too late.'' Hassan cautiously followed the narrow road around a sharp curve, looking for the source of the impact up ahead. He found it two hundred yards further on.

The pickup truck that had passed them was tilted drunkenly on the side of the road. Its whole front end was smashed as if a giant hand had slammed down on it, compressing it to scrap metal. Across the road from it, a small gray sedan had stopped in the oncoming lane of traffic.

Hassan gave the gray car a quick glance. ''The sedan

doesn't seem to have been involved. I think the truck hit that tree.'' He pointed to a huge oak beside the road. The bottom part of its trunk gleamed whitely where the impact had striped away its bark.

''Call 911. Tell them to send an ambulance,'' he ordered.

Kali hurriedly made the call as Hassan carefully pulled up behind the wreck.

''Stay in the car,'' he said over his shoulder as he jumped out of the car.

''Not on your life.'' Kali determinedly followed him. ''I might be able to help you. I can at least make sure you don't get hit by oncoming traffic.''

Hassan gave her a frustrated look, but he didn't stop to argue. He raced across the road toward the sedan, which contained a white-faced teenager.

''Did he hit you?'' Hassan demanded.

The girl shook her head. ''No. He hit the tree. He—'' She gulped.

''Listen to me. I need your help.'' Hassan's calm voice seemed to steady the girl. ''First, you have to move your car completely off the road. In the trunk of my car are flares. I want you to get them and set them up on both sides of the accident, but keep away from the traffic while you do it. Understand?''

The girl nodded. ''Flares in the trunk. Both sides of the road.''

''And keep away from traffic,'' Hassan repeated as he shoved his car keys into her hand. ''When you've done that, I want you to go over to that stone fence,'' he pointed to a spot well away from the accident, ''and wait for the police to come.''

Without waiting to see if she was going to obey, Hassan grabbed Kali's arm and hustled her across the road toward the wrecked truck.

Wrenching open the door on the driver's side, he bent over the figure slumped against the steering wheel. Reaching inside, he pulled out the driver.

Staggering over to the side of the road, Hassan deposited the burly man on the grassy verge.

Kali trailed after him, eager to help but not sure how to do it.

"He doesn't look any too good," she stated the obvious.

"Have you got one of those disposable plastic ballpoint pens in your purse?" Hassan demanded.

"Yes," Kali said, wondering what was so important he needed to write it down now.

"Get it and hurry!"

Kali ran as fast as she could back to the Mercedes, snatched up her purse and upended it on her seat. Finding the pen, she raced back to Hassan and shoved it at him.

"Sit down with your legs stretched out in front of you," he ordered, pulling a Swiss army knife out of his pocket.

Kali didn't bother to ask why. Hassan seemed to know what he was doing, which was more than she did.

Hassan lifted the man, hastily positioning his head so that Kali's thigh provided a brace. While Kali watched, Hassan broke the pen in half, ripped out the ink cartridge and flung it aside.

Muttering something in his own language that she didn't understand but which sounded like a prayer to her, Hassan bent over the man. Using his knife, he cut a small incision in the man's throat and carefully worked the empty pen tube into the opening.

"Come on, damn you," Hassan muttered. "Breathe."

"Please, God," Kali sent up her own prayer. "No one deserves to die for stupidity."

After several agonizing seconds, the man suddenly made a gurgling noise, like a water faucet full of air.

"Where the hell is that ambulance?" Hassan muttered.

As if in answer to his query, Kali heard the faint sound of a siren in the distance.

"Is he going to be all right?" Kali asked uncertainly, not sure just what Hassan had done. They hadn't covered anything like that in the first aid course she'd taken. Could he have learned more exotic first aid because in his own country, doctors were harder to come by? But he didn't live in his own country. He lived in America and had since college. Although his Ph.D. was in biology. Maybe they covered things like that in doctoral-level courses? That could explain it.

"He's breathing, and that sure beats the hell out of not breathing, but..." Hassan's eyes dropped to the man's chest, and he sighed. There was a faint circle outlined in blood across the man's gray T-shirt as if he'd hit the steering wheel with a great deal of force.

Kali echoed Hassan's sigh. Not only had the man been driving like a maniac, but he hadn't been wearing a seat belt, either.

The ambulance skidded to a stop behind them in a shower of gravel. Two men jumped out and rushed over to them.

"What d'you got?" One of them asked as he fell to his knees beside them.

"Probable crushed larynx," Hassan said.

The man whistled. "That's as neat an emergency tracheotomy as I've ever seen. Don't move for just a few minutes longer, lady, while I replace that piece of plastic you used, and then we'll load him in the ambulance.

"He have any passengers?" the second medical technician asked with a quick glance at the truck.

"No," Hassan said.

"There. That should hold until we can get him to the hospital," the first technician said. "Let's get him into the ambulance, Joe."

They were in the process of putting the man into the ambulance just as the state police car arrived. The officer hurried over to the ambulance.

"You folks all right?" the trooper asked.

"We're fine, Officer," Hassan answered him. "We were right behind him when the accident happened. But that poor kid over there," he nodded to the girl who was sitting forlornly on the stone fence, "is pretty upset. She shouldn't drive."

"Don't worry. I'll radio for someone to take her home. Hell, this kind of thing upsets *me,* and I've been on the force twenty years. If you'll just give me your names and addresses, you can go."

Fear sent a shaft of adrenaline through Hassan. Giving his name would expose his impersonation. Kali would find out the truth and not only would she be furious with him, but she'd also feel humiliated. And she didn't deserve that.

He glanced at her, feeling a sense of pride at the way she was handling all this.

"Kali, would you give him your name and address? I want to thank the girl for her help with the flares."

Kali instinctively checked the road for traffic as Hassan started across it.

"That's a good man to have on your side in an emergency," the medic said, claiming Kali's attention. "If it hadn't been for him, the driver would have been dead by now.''

''He's a good man to have on your side anytime,'' Kali said, rather surprised to find that she meant it with all her heart. She'd always respected Hassan's intelligence and liked him as a person. But she would never have described him as a good man in an emergency, which he was. He'd known exactly what had to be done and how to do it.

''Thank you, Dr. Whitman,'' the policeman said, once she'd given him her name and address. Closing his notebook, he waited until Hassan returned and then said, ''Someone will be in touch with you tomorrow to get the full particulars. I don't think we'll need your help, sir, since your fiancée has already supplied a fairly detailed account.''

''Come on, Kali.'' Hassan put his arm around Kali's shoulders and urged her toward the Mercedes.

The weight of his arm felt comforting, as if it were a bulwark against the dangers of the outside world—a very dangerous world where disaster sometimes struck without warning.

She glanced back at the twisted hunk of metal that just a short time before had been a truck.

She shivered, remembering the pale blue features of the man Hassan had fought so hard to save.

Kali hastily gathered the contents of her purse off the seat and shoved it back inside before getting into the car. She stared down at her clenched fists, gritting her teeth against the tears clogging her throat. She absolutely refused to burst into tears like some die-away Victorian miss. Especially not now when it was all over.

She heard the sound of the car door slamming behind Hassan and then the murmur of his voice saying something, but it sounded indistinct as if it were coming from a great distance. Finally it evaporated into nothingness, and for the first time in her life Kali fainted.

Hassan hastily made her comfortable and buckled her in and then carefully pulled out into the road. He wanted to get her back to the security of her apartment as soon as possible, where he was going to tell her that not only wasn't he Karim, but that Karim didn't want her anymore. Hassan swore succinctly in Arabic under his breath.

The forcefully delivered words penetrated the fog surrounding Kali. She opened her eyes to find herself staring at Hassan's cleanly chiseled profile.

''Me, too,'' she muttered.

''You, too, what?''

''I haven't the vaguest idea what you're saying, but it sounds just like I feel,'' she mumbled. ''What's the language? Arabic?''

''Yes.'' Hassan shot her a quick glance. ''How do you feel?''

''Did I faint?'' she asked incredulously.

''Dead away.'' Hassan winced at his inadvertent choice of words. ''Close your eyes and rest until we get back to your apartment.''

And don't bother me? Kali wondered at the curtness of his tone. Nevertheless she obediently closed her eyes. Could he have been disgusted by her weakness in fainting? Uncertainly she chewed on her lower lip. Could her having fainted on top of the afternoon they'd endured be giving him second thoughts about the wisdom of marrying her?

Kali tried to ignore the sudden flare of panic she felt. It didn't matter if he did call off the wedding, she tried to tell herself. There were no deep emotions involved on

JUDITH McWILLIAMS   57

either side. It shouldn't matter to her if he backed out. But even though it shouldn't matter, it did. It mattered very much.

Kali leaned her head back against the seat to try to figure out why and promptly fell asleep.

Hassan heard her even breathing with satisfaction. Not only was sleep was the best thing for her at the moment, but the silence would allow him to figure out the best way to break his news to her.

Maybe he should start his explanation by telling her that he wasn't Karim? He was his twin. She might be so mad about his impersonation that she wouldn't care so much about the broken engagement.

Hassan frowned as he remembered the obnoxious Bart. Kali would care all right when she had to go home and tell her family that Karim had broken their engagement. She'd probably have to listen to Bart say he told her so for the rest of her life.

There had to be some way to break the engagement so that Kali didn't appear to be rejected in her family's eyes. He mulled over the problem as he sped along the highway.

By the time they arrived at her apartment, he still hadn't come up with an idea that would silence Bart.

Kali opened her eyes as he pulled into a parking space. She blinked at him, reminding him of a small, dignified owl.

"Sorry," she muttered. "I can't think what's the matter with me."

"Stress." Hassan got out and walked around the car to open her door.

"I have plenty of stress in my life, and I've never

reacted to it by falling asleep before,'' she said as she followed him into the lobby.

"In an emergency the body produces excess amounts of adrenaline and when the emergency fades so does the adrenaline, leaving you feeling wiped out.'' Hassan listened to his pedantic explanation with a sense of disbelief. How could he be lecturing her about physiology when what he wanted to do was to take her in his arms and tell her that she'd been absolutely magnificent? To assure her that just because his brother didn't want to marry her didn't mean that there weren't plenty of men who would.

In fact, if he weren't committed to returning to the Middle East, he'd give serious thought to applying for the position himself. But he was committed, he reminded himself, and there was no way Kali could ever be happy living in his father's kingdom. No way any normal Western woman would put up with always having to wear a veil in public, at being denied an education or a career, at not being allowed to drive a car or even to leave her home without a male relative in attendance.

Silently Hassan followed her up to her apartment and waited nervously while she unlocked the door.

Tell her quickly, he urged himself once they were inside. Just blurt it out and get it over with.

Bracing himself, he took a deep breath, but before he could get the words out, Kali reached up and placed her soft lips against his. He trembled at the unexpected kiss. Her lips felt so warm and soft and alluring. And the faint floral fragrance she was wearing drifted through his mind, tangling his thoughts into an incoherent mass.

Tell her! his mind screamed at him, but his body was far too busy enjoying the kiss to pay any attention.

"You, Hassan Rashid, are one very special man. I've

never seen anyone who was as cool as you were in an emergency.''

He wasn't so cool now, he thought. Much hotter and he'd be in danger of spontaneous combustion. And it was all wrong. How could he be enjoying kissing her so much when he was about to tell her that his brother had rejected her?

"Hassan?" Kali stared at him, confused by his continued silence.

"What?" She clutched his arm in sudden fear. "You didn't hurt yourself back there, did you?"

"No," he muttered. "I just... I mean... You see—"

Hassan gulped, unable to get out a complete sentence, let alone one that said what he had to say. He couldn't do it. He just couldn't do it to her. Not immediately after the stress of the accident.

"I'd better go home and clean up," he mumbled, offering the first excuse that came to mind. "I'll give you a call tomorrow," he added as he left.

Kali shut the door behind him, trying to shake the feeling that he was escaping from her. Don't turn paranoid, she told herself. It's probably just his way of reacting to the stress of the evening. You fell asleep, so he went home and...

And what? she wondered as she headed toward the shower. What did Hassan do to unwind?

She didn't know, but she was very much looking forward to finding out.

Hassan breathed a sigh of relief when the elevator doors closed behind him. Coward, he castigated himself. *You agreed to tell Kali, and you've never shrunk from an unpleasant task before.*

He jabbed the down button in frustration. The problem

was that Kali had inexplicably become far more than just another unpleasant mess of Karim's to clean up. She was a person whom he liked. A lot.

He didn't want to hurt her. But how he felt didn't matter, he reminded himself. The cold, hard fact was that Karim had married someone else. In two weeks he would be back in New York with his bride, and there would be no way to keep it from Kali.

Hassan's eyes narrowed as he suddenly realized something. He did have those two weeks. Two weeks might be long enough for Kali to decide on her own that she didn't want to marry his brother.

Hassan carefully considered the idea. If Kali were the one to reject Karim, then not only would he be spared having to tell her the truth, but she also would be able to tell her family that this time she had been the one to break her engagement. She would feel as if she'd had a lucky escape instead of feeling humiliated.

Yes, that was it. He bit back his sudden flare of excitement, trying to think.

He had to be back in Boston by tomorrow morning, and his time was totally committed until Wednesday afternoon. But after that, he could arrange to be free until the following Monday.

All he had to do was to figure out what would make Kali break her engagement. He pondered the problem as he drove home.

Maybe if he were to exhibit a personal trait that annoyed her so much she wouldn't feel she couldn't live with it? But what?

Of course. He smiled in grim satisfaction. The simple truth would do. All he had to do was to give Kali a clear picture of just how restrictive being married to a man from his culture would be. He probably wouldn't even need the whole weekend to accomplish his goal. The thought, however, brought him no satisfaction.

Four

Hassan pressed the bridge of his nose between his thumb and forefinger, trying to push back the tiredness caused by three days of nonstop work. But it had been worth it because now he had a four-day weekend to spend with Kali.

"Did the consulate contact you with the information I asked for, Achmed?" Hassan asked Karim's houseman.

"Yes, Excellency."

"Good. Give me the details while I change." Hassan took off his suit jacket and dropped it on the couch as he headed toward the bedroom.

Achmed made a disapproving sound and hastily snatched it up before trotting after Hassan.

"There is a lecture about the place of women in the Arab world tonight at nine o'clock at The Church of the Resurrection on the Upper West Side behind the Museum of Natural History. Mohammed said to tell you that reservations were not necessary.

"But I cannot believe that you will enjoy it, Excellency," Achmed added gloomily. "Mohammed said the woman giving it spent two years in Saudi Arabia finding fault with everything."

"The lecture isn't supposed to be entertaining. It's supposed to be informative." To Kali, he thought.

A first-hand account by a typical Western woman of how stifling she'd found living in the Middle East should give Kali serious doubts about the wisdom of marrying an Arab. Then all he would have to do would be to reinforce her doubts by behaving like a stereotypical, Hollywood sheik, and by the time the weekend was over Kali would be only too eager to break her engagement.

Hassan's stomach suddenly rumbled as if to remind him that all he'd eaten today was a stale bagel for breakfast.

"Did you make reservations for dinner?" Hassan asked.

"Certainly. For six-thirty at your brother's favorite restaurant."

Not a comforting thought, Hassan thought, remembering a few of the restaurants in the past that had enjoyed Karim's favor. And rarely because of the caliber of the food they served.

"And His Highness called earlier and asked to speak to you."

"Dad called? Did he leave a message?" Hassan yanked off his tie and tossed it toward the bed.

Achmed caught it in midair.

"He said he tried Boston first, but you'd already left for the airport. He requested that you call him back as soon as you arrived in New York.'' Achmed held out his hand for Hassan's suit pants.

"Thanks, that'll be all.'' Hassan waited until Achmed had left the room and then picked up the phone. Five minutes and two secretaries later, he was connected with his father.

"Hassan, lad. How are you?''

"Fine, sir. Achmed said you wanted to speak to me?''

"Yes, about two things, actually. First, I wanted to let you know that we ran into some problems over the staffing of that new pediatric hospital we're going to open next month.''

Hassan tried to ignore the sudden suffocating sense of panic that filled him. "I can cut my course in hospital management short and come home now,'' he offered.

"No, don't do that, lad. I think having you finish the course will be more beneficial to us in the long run. It plus your medical degree should enable you to handle just about anything that comes up.''

Hassan felt his muscles relax at the reprieve he'd just been given. It wasn't that he didn't want to go back to Saad Dev'a to live, he assured himself. It was just that he wanted to do as much good as possible when he did return and to do that he needed to learn a whole lot more than he already knew.

"I was able to hire the grandson of Fayed's cousin to look after things until you can get here. The boy's been working in hospital management for the past ten years in London, and was unexpectedly laid off in a cost-cutting measure last week. He was quite glad to take the job on a temporary basis.''

"Good,'' Hassan said. "If he doesn't pan out let me know.''

"Pan... Oh, you mean do the job. Yes, I will. Now, about the other matter..."

Hassan instinctively braced himself at the odd note in his father's voice.

"Remember when you were here last summer, you said that you intended to take a wife when you returned to stay?"

"Yes." Hassan shrugged his shoulders as if trying to dislodge a weight that was becoming uncomfortably heavy.

"Well, last evening after prayers I was talking to Suleiman ibn Yaki, and he suggested that you might be interested in marrying his oldest daughter."

"No!" Hassan instinctively blurted the denial out.

"But, Hassan, this girl sounds ideal. Suleiman assures me she's quite pretty, she's distantly related to us, and she knows what would be expected of her in marriage."

As I know what is expected of me, Hassan reminded himself. Marriage to a woman of the kingdom was his duty. He knew it. He opened his mouth to agree, but the words wouldn't come.

"How about if I tell Suleiman that you aren't quite ready to marry yet?" his father finally suggested as the silence lengthened.

"Thanks, Dad. I'll call you next week." Hassan hastily hung up, feeling as if he'd just dodged a bullet.

All he could think about was a spy movie he'd seen as a kid in which the hero had been trapped in a corridor where the walls were slowly inching together, threatening to crush the life out of him. He felt as if he were the one in that corridor, anchored there by the twin chains of duty and his long-ago promise to his father.

"Is something wrong, Excellency?"

Hassan jumped at the sound of Achmed's worried voice.

"No! No," Hassan repeated, moderating his voice.

There was nothing wrong with his not wanting to marry a woman whose first name he didn't even know, he assured himself. Nor was it wrong that he bitterly regretted having to give up the practice of pediatrics, which he found so deeply satisfying, for hospital administration, which he found boring. A bit selfish, perhaps, but not wrong.

What would be wrong would be his acting on his reluctance by refusing to honor his commitments. And he had no intention of doing that. He would do his duty.

Hassan got to his feet and headed into the shower, refusing to delve any deeper into his growing aversion to returning to the Middle East.

Kali adjusted her silver heart pendant so that it rested precisely in the middle of the deeply scooped neckline of her new green silk dress. She ran her hand down over her full skirt and then twisted around to check the fit in the back. The sleek material fell smoothly over her slender hips.

"Perfect," she pronounced in satisfaction. The dress was worth every penny of the outrageous price she'd paid for it.

Grabbing the bottle of lavender scent from her dresser, she headed out to the kitchen.

"Lavender and pumpkin," Kali murmured, rechecking the magazine article she'd left on the kitchen counter. It seemed a strange combination of scents to be an aphrodisiac, but according to the article the tests had been carried out by a reputable university. And the results had left no room for ambiguity. The scent of lavender mixed with pumpkin was sexier to men than any perfume the researchers had tested.

And an aphrodisiac was exactly what she wanted. Kali swallowed against the sudden flare of excitement making her stomach churn.

Her need to make love to Hassan had been growing ever since his return and now it was all she seemed able to think about. It was almost as if someone had programmed her mind with an erotic fantasy and set it to go off at random intervals. And while her fantasy made riding the bus a lot more interesting than ever before, it had also increased her frustration level. Her nerves felt like they'd been stretched to the breaking point.

Kali grimaced. She wished she could simply ask Hassan to make love to her, but she couldn't quite work up the courage to do it. While she didn't think he would find such a request wrong, she wasn't sure enough to risk it. His Middle-Eastern background was such an unknown quantity. Most of the time she forgot he wasn't an American, but every once in a while he did or said something that reminded her.

And while she could easily deal with small anomalies in the way each of them looked at the world, what worried her was that hidden beneath the surface of those small differences was a great big difference. One so fundamental that it would sabotage their engagement. And it didn't get much more fundamental than how one looked at sex. And that being so, she intended to tread very carefully. At least until after they were married.

"Research or not, pumpkin and lavender sounds weird," she muttered as she opened the can of pumpkin and studied the bright orange pulp.

"Faint heart never won sexy man," she encouraged herself.

Determinedly she sprayed lavender on herself and then, dipping her fingertip into the pumpkin, rubbed some of it behind each ear where she hoped it wouldn't be visible. Pumpkin orange would clash with the green of her dress.

She was trying to decide if she should apply more pumpkin and, if so, where, when the doorbell chimed. She glanced at the clock, frowning slightly.

She'd found a message from someone named Achmed on her answering machine yesterday evening, saying that Hassan would pick her up for dinner at six-thirty tonight. It was almost that time now. But Hassan was never on time.

Except Sunday, she suddenly remembered. He had been on time when he'd picked her up to go to Eddie's christening. Maybe he was making an effort to be punctual to please her? If so, it was working. If she were much more pleased with him, she'd be all over him.

Kali swung the door open, and a wave of intense pleasure surged through her at the sight of Hassan standing on her doorstep. He looked absolutely gorgeous in his dark gray suit. Like a sexy spy taken from the pages of a modern-day thriller.

To her surprise, instead of giving her a casually friendly hello as he normally did, he suddenly swept her up in his arms. He pressed his lips against hers as if he were as starved for physical contact between them as she was.

Kali trembled as she felt the pressure of his tongue against her lips demanding entrance. Eagerly she opened them, and he shoved his tongue inside to explore the warm cavern of her mouth. Waves of excitement poured through her, and Kali threaded her fingers through his crisp black hair, relishing its silky texture. His head felt warm and hard beneath her caressing fingertips. And she could feel a similar hardness beginning to be reflected elsewhere in his body.

To her intense disappointment, instead of deepening their intimacy Hassan released her, suddenly seeming to be as eager to get away from her as he had originally been to kiss her.

Kali took what comfort she could from the faint tremor she could see in his fingers as he pushed back the hair she'd disheveled. He might have broken off their kiss, but he clearly hadn't been unaffected by it.

Hassan fumbled through the haze of sexual desire clogging his mind, looking for something to say.

"That's a nice dress," he finally said, and then winced at the anemic-sounding compliment.

That wasn't what he wanted to say. He wanted to tell her that she looked fantastic in it. That when he saw her wearing it he wanted to sweep her up in his arms and carry her off to bed.

It was a good thing he couldn't get the words out, he told himself. He had no business even thinking about making love to Kali, let alone saying it. It was bad enough that he couldn't seem to stop himself from kissing her, but making love to her when she thought he was his brother would be highly unethical. And it would be impossible once she found out he wasn't. The knowledge depressed him.

The plan. He snatched at it like a lifeline. *Concentrate on convincing her that you are a closet male chauvinist.*

"We need to hurry. I have reservations at that new restaurant everyone's talking about," he said.

Now he sounded like himself, Kali thought as she slipped into her coat.

* * *

The volume from the live band hit Kali with the force of a slap when she entered the restaurant. They sounded like they were playing warmup for the Tower of Babel.

Marriage was a series of compromises, and Hassan liked the social scene, Kali reminded herself as she followed their hostess through the crowded restaurant.

The woman stopped beside a tiny table on the edge of the postage-stamp dance area directly in front of the band, placed their menus on the table and with a distracted smile left.

Kali sank into her chair and smiled gamely at Hassan, trying to remember if she had any aspirin in her purse. An hour of this and she was going to need some.

Hassan smiled back, trying not to wince as the raucous music battered his tired mind.

"We were very lucky to get a table here." His smile of pseudosatisfaction was belied by the muscle below his left eye that twitched in mute protest when the drummer suddenly increased his volume, seemingly in a futile attempt to drown out his fellow musicians.

"What?" Kali leaned toward him in an effort to hear him.

Hassan scooted his chair closer to her and, putting his mouth near her ear, whispered, "I said we were very lucky to get…" He completely lost track of what he had been going to say when the most tantalizing aroma he'd ever smelled drifted into his lungs. It was soft and sensuous, reminding him of starlit nights and sun-dabbled beaches. An image of Kali running naked over the sand flittered through his mind. White sand clung to her slender hips and dusted her firm breasts with a diamond glitter. He'd—

Better remember why he was with her in the first place! He jerked back as if he'd been stabbed.

Kali studied his taut features, wondering if his abrupt reaction was a result of smelling her lavender and pumpkin concoction. If it was, there was no telling how the evening might end.

She made an effort to suppress her sudden excitement, telling herself that it was premature. His reaction could be nothing more than the fact that he was tired and off balance. But how could she find out which it was?

Her eyes strayed to the dance floor. It should be easy enough to lure him out there, and once there she could snuggle close enough to give him a good whiff of her lavender and pumpkin. Then she should be able to judge his reaction to it.

The fact that this place was so crowded would work to her advantage. She would be able to plaster herself up against him without him thinking anything more than that they didn't have room for more conventional dancing.

Happily she opened her menu, hoping the food was tolerable. Not only was she hungry, but she would need to keep up her strength for the activities she had in mind once she got him back to her apartment.

Making herself understood to the waiter, who was either wearing earplugs in self-defense or who had been rendered hard of hearing by the noise, was not easy. Finally she simply pointed to her choices and hoped that she would get something she could eat.

Once the waiter had left, Kali leaned across the table and mouthed the word, "Dance?"

Hassan blinked in dismay as he suddenly remembered that Karim loved to dance. And he didn't. Couldn't, in fact. The term "two left feet" might have been coined to describe his efforts at dancing.

But he wished he could. He stared into Kali's bright

brown eyes. He wanted to be able to hold her close, even if it was in a public place and even though he knew that nothing could ever come of it.

Frantically he tried to decide what to do. If he indulged his craving to hold her, then she'd be able to tell that he couldn't dance and that would make her suspicious if she knew how Karim danced. On the other hand, what excuse could he offer in refusal? He could hardly say he was too tired, when the whole point of his bringing Kali here was to convince her that he was the kind of man who found his relaxation in organized mayhem.

His only real option was to try to bluff it out, he finally decided.

The band switched to a slower, although no less loud, selection, and Hassan got to his feet. Holding out his hand to Kali, he guided her to a tiny open spot on the dance floor.

Kali snuggled into his arms with an unselfconscious pleasure that filled him with a confusing mixture of lust and tenderness. She felt so good. Like a fantasy come to life. A fantasy he hadn't even been aware he'd had.

He took a deep breath, filling his lungs with the intoxicating aroma that surrounded her, trying to identify the elusive scent. He couldn't. All he was sure of was that it was the sexiest perfume he'd ever run across.

A sharp jab in his back from someone behind him reminded him that he was supposed to be dancing. He began to shuffle his feet in the hope that if he didn't actually lift them off the floor, he wouldn't step on Kali's feet. That was the usual fate of any woman unlucky enough to be his partner.

Kali nestled her head against his shoulder, savoring the muscular feel of his hard body. He had the most fantastic physique. All muscle. There didn't appear to be an ounce of fat on him. She just wished he didn't have anything else on him. Like clothes.

Her heartbeat sped up at the intoxicating thought of Hassan naked. What would he look like?

"Our dinner's here," Hassan spoke in her ear.

"What?" Kali pretended not to hear and pressed herself a little closer to him.

Stepping back, he took her arm and used his body to force a path between the packed dancers.

To Kali's surprise the food was delicious, and she started to eat with the appetite of someone who'd missed lunch and only had coffee for breakfast.

Hassan surreptitiously studied her, faintly confused by her reaction to this place. Kali was a serious-minded, highly intelligent woman who should find all this noise and confusion as unsettling as he did. So why hadn't she complained about it? Or for that matter why hadn't she even seemed to notice his lack of skill in dancing?

He didn't know, and that worried him.

Uneasily he picked up his fork and started to eat since the noise level made conversation an impossibility.

"And...your...dessert?"

Hassan stared up at their waiter, having heard about every fifth word the man had said.

"Dessert?" The waiter finally made himself understood by pointing to the dessert menu.

Hassan was about to ask Kali if she wanted dessert when he remembered his role. He wasn't supposed to be giving her choices. He was supposed to be dictatorial.

Hassan emphatically shook his head at the waiter and then glanced at Kali to see how she was reacting to his high-handedness at depriving her of a sweet.

To his confusion, instead of being annoyed, she gave him an approving smile.

Hassan hastily signed the check the waiter gave him, took his receipt and then hustled Kali out of the restaurant.

Kali took a sniff of the cold, bracing air that hit them when they finally squeezed past the people waiting in the entrance for a table.

She wrinkled her nose and sniffed again. "It smells like snow."

"You needn't sound so happy about it." Hassan helped her into her coat, since there hadn't been room inside for her to put it on.

"I like snow."

Hassan peered down into her eyes, which were sparkling with the reflection from the streetlights. She looked adorable. And eminently kissable.

Clenching his hands into fists to keep from grabbing her, Hassan took a deep breath and announced, "We're going to a lecture at a church over behind the Museum of Natural History about a woman's place in Middle-Eastern society. I thought you would find it informative."

Hassan studied her face trying to judge her reaction to his statement. He couldn't. She looked politely interested. Nothing more.

"The lecture should help you understand my background," he added in case she'd missed the point.

"It sounds interesting," she said.

But before Hassan could hail a cab, a man came up behind them, pointing a gun. "Hand over your wallet and your Rolex, buddy. And I want that ring you're wearing, too, sister."

"But it's my engagement ring!" Kali protested.

"So he buys you another one. Come on!"

Kali winced as the man suddenly grabbed her, his fingers tightening painfully around her wrist.

"Give it to me." The assailant fumbled for her ring with his free hand.

Without warning Hassan's left hand smashed down on the gun a second before the edge of his right hand impacted at the base of the thug's neck with a dull thud.

Kali watched in disbelief as the man crumpled to the sidewalk like a balloon that had suddenly lost all its air.

She gulped and looked at Hassan, her mind a confusing jumble of what might have happened.

"You should never argue with people who are pointing guns at you," she muttered distractedly.

"He was hurting you. Look at your wrist."

Kali looked. The marks made by the man's fingers stood out as reddish blotches on her pale skin.

"By tomorrow morning those will be bruises." Hassan glanced malevolently down at the unconscious man, and Kali shivered.

Hassan looked nothing like his normal, easygoing self. He looked like a picture she'd once seen of an Eastern potentate condemning a group of prisoners to death. And yet this unexpected facet of his personality didn't scare her. On the contrary, it gave her a sense of security to know that he was physically capable of protecting her from muggers.

But she couldn't let herself forget that just because her feelings for him were growing by the minute didn't mean that he felt more for her now than he had when he'd originally proposed marriage. The truth depressed her.

"Safe." Hassan breathed a sigh of relief as a cab pulled up.

With one last glance at the mugger who had staggered

to his feet and was shaking his head as if trying to figure out what happened, she climbed into the cab. Kali wondered how her life could have become so muddled in just a few short days. Everything had seemed so straightforward when he'd originally asked her to marry him. She'd liked Hassan's personality, respected his mind and shared many of his goals. Sex had been a very minor part of the original equation.

So why was her every second thought now of the pleasures to be found in bed with him? She couldn't come up with a single feasible answer. All she knew for certain was that ever since he'd returned from his trip to Australia, she'd seen him differently. As if his personality had suddenly come into focus and her clearer vision had heightened her feelings for him to the point where they were in danger of becoming obsessive. It didn't make a lot of sense, but then very little about sexual attraction could be explained logically, she reminded herself.

Hassan absently rubbed his right hand against his thigh as the cab sped away from the curb.

For the first time in his life he began to have an inkling of just what Karim meant when he said that living on the edge was fun. Tonight really had been fun in a weird sort of way.

But had it done anything to advance his goal of getting Kali to break her engagement? He shot a quick glance at her. She was staring straight ahead, seemingly lost in her own thoughts.

He didn't know her well enough to predict how she'd allocate the blame for this evening's fiasco. There was more than enough of it to go around.

The problem was that around Kali he tended to do a

lot more feeling than thinking, which was totally unlike him.

Hassan shifted uneasily at the thought.

"Does your hand hurt?" Kali noticed his expression.

"Hurt? No, why should it?"

"You mean just because you hit that overgrown delinquent hard enough to knock him out?"

"It doesn't hurt if you do it right."

"But I don't know how to do it at all, let alone right. Will you teach me?"

"It takes a lot of practice," Hassan hedged, fighting to keep his voice casual as his body instinctively reacted to the images that flooded his mind at the thought of teaching her some of the more exotic holds.

"I'd still like to learn. You can give me my first lesson tonight after the lecture." Kali tried not to sound too eager. She didn't know what was involved in learning what appeared to be a form of martial art, but common sense said it was bound to involve a lot of physical contact. And who knew where physical contact might lead? Especially with her providing every bit of encouragement she could.

Giving in to her growing need to touch him, she ran her hand over the shoulder of his suit jacket, ostensibly to smooth out the wrinkles in the material. His body felt so firm and solid beneath her fingers. Much like Hassan's personality was turning out to be.

And he was all hers. Kali struggled to contain the sudden surge of impatience she felt. She didn't want to waste her evening listening to some woman talk about her experiences in life; she wanted to work on a few experiences of her own.

Five

"I guess we just follow the arrows," Hassan said once they were in the church hall's vestibule.

Skirting a group of women who were reading something on the bulletin board to the right of the entrance, he started down the dimly lit hallway.

"Who's sponsoring this talk?" Kali asked.

"I have no idea. Why?"

"Because it helps to know where the lecturer is coming from so you can consider it when you're listening to what they have to say. For example, if I go to a talk on gun control sponsored by the NRA I'm going to hear a very different slant on the subject than if I listen to one given by the mother of a child killed while he was playing with a gun he picked up at a friend's house."

"True," Hassan conceded. "But some facts will remain the same no matter who's telling them."

"There speaks the eternal optimist," Kali gave him

an impish grin that sent a shaft of pure desire spiraling
through him.

Desire that faded as quickly as it had flared leaving
behind a sense of loneliness. He wasn't an optimist, he
thought. He was a realist. A realist who knew that he
was committed to returning to the Middle East. No
amount of optimistic thinking and no woman, no matter
how enticing she was, could change those facts.

Kali looked at his closed face, wondering why her
teasing comment should have caused such a reaction.

Unless he knew that the organization sponsoring the
talk was opposed to Middle Eastern-Western marriages?
But if that were the case then why would he bring her
to the lecture in the first place?

"You'd better hurry. The lecture is about to start," a
middle-aged woman standing by the door to the auditorium told them.

Regretfully Kali dropped what had promised to be an
intriguing line of discussion and entered the room.

She stood for a moment just inside the doors while
her eyes adjusted to the dimmer lighting, studying the
audience.

"They seem to have a pretty good turnout," she said
to Hassan as she sat in one of the empty seats near the
back.

"That's because it's required attendance for anyone
enrolled in a couple of the women's study courses over
at Columbia," the young woman in the seat beside
Kali's told her.

The woman's eyes moved past Kali to study Hassan
with a frank curiosity that annoyed Kali. She didn't want
her looking at Hassan as if he were a particularly tooth-
some treat they'd just discovered.

Jealousy is the mark of a small mind, Kali told herself,

but the thought didn't do a thing to alleviate the uncomfortable feeling. Small-minded or not, she wanted to post No Trespassing signs all over Hassan.

Kali forced herself to concentrate as the moderator walked on the stage to introduce the main speaker. She really was curious to learn more about the culture that had shaped Hassan.

Ten minutes into the woman's speech, Kali reached the conclusion that the lecture wasn't about the differences between the cultures; it was about the irrationality of a woman in love.

Another hour's worth of the woman's rambling, self-pitying monologue only deepened Kali's initial opinion. Finally the woman finished, and the moderator opened the floor to questions.

"I don't have any questions," she whispered to Hassan. "Let's get out of here."

Hassan obediently stepped into the aisle, ignoring the accusatory looks his Arab features garnered from a few members of the audience as he escorted Kali out of the auditorium.

"What did you think of the lecture?" he forced himself to ask.

"That wasn't a lecture, it was a diatribe. Or a monument."

Hassan blinked uncertainly. "Monument?"

"To the stupidity of a woman in love!" Kali shook her head. "It never fails to amaze me how being in love can turn an otherwise rational person into a raving lunatic. It makes me all the gladder that I'm going to marry you."

Hassan stared at her, completely dumbfounded by her words. They didn't make any sense. She'd just spent an hour listening to a fellow Western woman outline in excruciating detail every horror that could befall a modern woman living in the Middle East and instead of giving her second thoughts about marrying him, it made her glad?

"Why?" he finally asked.

"Because that woman is the perfect example of what happens when you decide to marry someone with your hormones instead of your head. She thought she was in love with some guy, so she calmly waltzes off to set up housekeeping in a foreign country without bothering to find out what she was getting into. Then when the novelty of being in love wore off, she suddenly couldn't stand it anymore, and she came running home crying about how horrible everything was.

"Thank heavens neither of us was blinded by our hormones when we made our decision to marry," Kali said.

"But that is my culture the woman was talking about," Hassan pointed out.

"But you don't live there. Your life is here in New York. From what that lady said, her husband never tried to hide the fact that he was intending to return to the Middle East once he got his graduate degree."

"Yes, but…"

"Not that she's unique in ignoring inconvenient facts," Kali admitted. "As you pointed out last Sunday, I no longer have anything in common with the first man I fell in love with."

"Yes," Hassan muttered, at a loss as to what he should do next. He'd expected that this lecture would convince her to break her engagement or, at the very least, give her serious doubts, and instead it appeared to have strengthened her determination to go through with the marriage.

Protectively he took her arm as he pushed open the church door.

The Middle Eastern male's attitude toward women wasn't all bad, Kali thought. They were very protective of their women. Much more so than the average Western men she'd dated.

Not that she needed protecting. At least, not most of the time, she amended honestly. But still it was nice to be cherished occasionally.

She climbed into the cab Hassan hailed and leaned back against the seat, immediately forgetting the lecture. She was far more interested in what would happen when they got back to her apartment, when Hassan gave her the promised lesson in self-defense.

Her sense of anticipation reached a fever pitch by the time the cab deposited them in front of her building.

Kali hurried across the lobby and into the elevator, trying to keep her growing excitement from showing.

"Would you like a cup of coffee before or after you give me my lesson?" Kali tried to forestall him changing his mind.

"Lesson?"

Kali refused to back down at his blank expression. She was beginning to feel as if she would go stark raving mad if she didn't at least get to kiss him properly, and she couldn't count on him instigating it himself. Not given the almost businesslike terms of their engagement.

"You said you'd teach me self-defense."

"Yes, I did, didn't I?" Hassan muttered, knowing that it was a bad idea but unable to bring himself to flatly refuse.

He glanced distractedly around the living room, trying

to decide what to do. "We need a mat to protect you when you fall," he said, in a halfhearted effort to stall.

A mat? Kali hastily swallowed a smile. He couldn't have provided a better opening if she'd given it to him.

"Yes, I can see we're going to need something soft for you to land on when I toss you," she said.

Hassan looked down his nose at her. "Optimistic thing, aren't you?" he quoted her words back at her.

"You'd better believe it," she said fervently. "And as for a mat, we can simply take the mattress off my bed, carry it out here and use it."

She tensed, waiting for his reaction. If he agreed, there was no telling what might happen.

"Mattress?" he repeated, his mind busily considering if he could somehow use a lesson in self-defense to further his goal of getting her to break her engagement. Maybe he could be dogmatic about the lesson? he considered. And impatient. If he were imperious on the heels of this evening's lecture, it might raise a few doubts in her. Doubts that he would be able to exploit.

"It's the only thing I've got in the apartment that's even close to a mat."

"Yes. Yes, you will learn self-defense," he added a little more emphatically, deciding to give it a try.

"That's what I said," Kali agreed absently, far more interested in his abstracted manner than what he was saying. Could it be that he wanted to make love to her, too, and was uncertain as to how she'd react if he tried? It was possible. It was also possible that he realized what she wanted and didn't share her desire, but didn't want to hurt her feelings.

Kali hastily shoved the deflating thought aside. Dwelling on negatives wouldn't help her reach her goal.

"Come on, let's get the mattress," she said.

Hassan obediently followed her into the bedroom.

Kali hurriedly stripped the bedding off the mattress and then helped Hassan lug it out to the living room where they dropped it in the middle of the floor.

"Okay, now what?" she asked.

"Well, I guess the first thing to do would be for us to take our shoes and socks off. Bare feet give you better traction."

Kali nodded.

Kicking off her shoes, she then peered down at her nylon-clad feet and then glanced over at Hassan who was pulling off his black dress socks and paying no attention to her.

Barefoot, he'd said. She tried to figure out how she could casually pull up her skirt and strip off her panty hose and failed utterly. It was not a casual kind of activity. It was a very intimate kind of activity. Although certainly not too intimate for an engaged couple. But then theirs wasn't a normal engagement, she reminded herself again. Not by any stretch of the imagination.

She took a deep, steadying breath. She wasn't going to get anywhere by dithering. The only way she'd succeed in deepening their intimacy was by pushing at his reserve...but gently, casually, as if her behavior were the most normal thing in the world. That way if he suddenly withdrew she wouldn't be terminally embarrassed.

"Turn around," she said.

Hassan looked up. "Opponents are supposed to face each other."

"I need to take my panty hose off, and that's a little more involved than you just pulling socks off."

"Oh," Hassan muttered and turned around, even though he didn't want to. He wanted to watch her lift the silky material of her skirt up. Up over the slim perfection of her legs. He wanted to feast his eyes on her soft skin. He wanted to run his fingers over her calf and explore the indentation behind her knee. He wanted to touch the satiny skin of her inner thigh.

Hassan closed his eyes in an agony of longing as he heard the silk of her dress rustle as she lifted it. He shouldn't feel this way, he tried to tell himself. He wasn't really her fiancé. He had no right to make love to her.

But it wasn't wrong to want to make love to her, he thought, rationalizing his feelings. It would only be wrong if he acted on his desire, and he wasn't going to do that. All he was going to do was to give her a lesson in self-defense. And that was a good idea. Everyone, particularly a beautiful woman living alone in a big city, should have some idea of how to defend themselves.

He turned when she told him to.

Kali was standing on the edge of the mattress, studying him with an intentness he found endearing. His lips twitched as he fought to contain a smile.

"What's so funny?" she asked.

"You. You look like you're trying to decide where to attack for the maximum effect."

"Why is that funny?" she took exception to his amusement. She wanted him to take her seriously. Very seriously.

"Because you haven't got a prayer." Unless… Hassan suddenly had his doubts. Kali was a very unpredictable woman. Full of surprises and hidden depths.

"Are you a martial arts expert?" he asked.

"Nope. I've always subscribed to the theory that one should avoid situations that call for a physical response. But tonight showed me that anyone can be in the wrong place at the wrong time.'' She tried to make her sudden desire to learn more about self-defense sound reasonable.

"Quite true. Why don't you try to attack me, and I'll show you how defense works.''

Now they were getting somewhere, Kali thought happily.

Speculatively she studied him. He looked enormous standing in the middle of her mattress. And totally impregnable. In a straight-up test of strength, she didn't stand a chance against him.

So if she couldn't outmuscle him, she'd just have to outwit him.

Glancing toward the window, she assumed a horrified expression and blurted out, "What's that?''

As she'd hoped, Hassan turned to see what she was looking at.

Knowing she would only have a second or two, she hurled herself at him, expecting to catch him off balance and tumble him to the floor. There she could use the weight of her body to hold him immobile long enough to claim a victory.

It didn't work. She landed against his chest, but he didn't budge. Not by so much as a centimeter.

Tentatively Kali wrapped her arms around his chest and squeezed. He still didn't move.

"What are you doing?'' He sounded no more than mildly curious.

Kali searched her memory of the class on self-defense she'd attended at the Y when she'd first moved to New York and came up with tripping. Trying to remember how the instructor had told them it should be done, she hooked her foot around his leg and shoved.

He went down all right, but that was the only part of her plan that went the way she'd envisioned. Kali wasn't quite sure how it happened, but instead of her being on top, she wound up beneath him.

Kali gasped as the intoxicating warmth of his muscular body engulfed her slighter frame, heating her blood and sending it singing through her veins.

She took a deep breath, trying to steady her skittering emotions and found instead that the scent of his cologne only intensified her reaction.

''Guile is a poor substitute for skill,'' Hassan's velvety voice floated over her head, encasing them in their own private world.

That shows what he knows, Kali thought, wiggling slightly in an attempt to free her arms so she could touch him. She couldn't. Her dress was caught between the mattress and his body, effectively pinning her arms down.

''My dress is stuck, and I don't have any freedom of movement,'' she complained. ''If it weren't for that, it would have worked.''

Hassan chuckled, and the movement pushed his chest into her breasts making them tingle.

''In the words of some philosopher or other, fat chance.''

''Would, too.''

Hassan propped himself on one elbow and stared into her challenging eyes.

Common sense told him that it was time for him to get up, say good-night and leave. But common sense didn't stand a chance against the sexual excitement building in him.

It would be all right, he assured himself. As long as he was aware of the potential danger of what they were doing, it would be all right. It wasn't like he was going to lose control. He never had before.

Even if he couldn't make love to her, there was nothing wrong with just kissing her. Nobody thought anything of a few kisses these days.

"What do you want to bet?" The challenge popped out without any conscious thought on his part.

"Bet?" Kali repeated, distracted by the movement of his lips as they formed the words. They had the most intriguingly sensual tilt.

"Just a little wager to add an incentive," he said.

"How about the first one to take a fall has to fix dinner one evening and no cheating by getting takeout?"

"Can you cook?" he asked.

"Ha! More to the point, can you? Now let me up so we can start even."

Hassan obligingly got to his feet.

Kali tried to still her racing heart as she slowly stood. She wanted to make love to him so much, and yet she was equally afraid of messing it up. Afraid that she was missing something that was vital to her future happiness. But she couldn't figure out what it could be.

You know he's a man, she encouraged herself, and you know he finds you sexually attractive. He hadn't been able to hide that fact, not when they'd been pressed together as closely as they had.

Deep in her thoughts, she stepped back. Her foot slipped off the edge of the mattress. Losing her balance, she tumbled sideways.

Kali landed against the coffee table, smacking her head on the edge of it.

She blinked, slightly dazed by the unexpected impact.

"Are you all right?" Hassan swept her up in his arms and set her down on the mattress.

"Let me see." He gently pushed back her hair and inspected the red mark on her temple.

"It's okay," she muttered. The feel of his warm body so close to her was driving out the slight pain in her head.

"Wood can cut like a knife," he insisted as his probing fingers moved slowly over her skin. "Fortunately it just seems to be an abrasion. It doesn't need a bandage."

"You could try the 'kiss it and make it better' cure," Kali murmured hopefully, her eyes lingering on his firm lips which were only inches from her face.

Her breath caught as they came closer and closer until they seemed to fill her entire range of vision. And then his mouth closed over hers, and she ceased to think at all and simply felt.

Her strangely provocative cologne drifted into Hassan's nostrils, heightening his awareness of her to near unbearable levels. He couldn't believe how good it felt to kiss her, to touch her. His hand inched up over her warm, silk-clad rib cage, and he shuddered at the longing that shafted through him when he felt the soft mound of her breast against his palm.

He wanted to push her dress aside and bare her breasts to his eyes. He wanted to kiss every single centimeter of their delicate flesh.

Unconsciously mating action to need, Hassan pushed his hand inside her deeply scooped neckline.

Her skin felt burning hot and velvety smooth. He closed his eyes the better to concentrate on the sensations building within him as his fingers inched up over the slope of her small breast to discover the turgid flesh of her nipple.

An agony of longing swept through him at the provocative feel of it brushing against his palm.

He wanted to—

No! he mentally screamed at himself. He couldn't

make love to her. It was wrong. He wasn't really engaged to her. She didn't even know who he was. He was supposed to be helping her, not taking advantage of her.

Disoriented and frustrated, he scrambled to his feet and blurted out, "I have to go. I forgot that I promised to check back at work on—"

For a horrible moment his mind went completely blank, and he couldn't remember what kind of work Karim did. Brain research, he finally remembered. That was it. Research.

"An experiment!" He listened to himself babble like a fool with a feeling of disbelief. What was the matter with him? It didn't matter, he decided. He could worry about it later. Right now he had to get away from Kali while he still could.

"I'll see you tomorrow night," he said over his shoulder as he rushed out of the apartment.

Kali listened to the door slam closed behind him, trying to figure out what had just happened. One second they'd been kissing, and the next he was practically running away. Why?

A tremor of unease shot through her as she remembered the lecture. The woman had claimed that Middle-Eastern men never rose above their culture's restrictive social and sexual mores. Even though Kali instinctively distrusted sweeping generalizations like that, it was possible that something in Hassan's background was responsible for his abrupt departure. If that was true, what else might be hidden there? It was a daunting thought that she didn't feel up to exploring at the moment.

Six

Hassan rushed out of Kali's apartment, feeling as if he were escaping from the scene of a crime. One that he had committed.

He rubbed his forehead with fingers that shook. All he'd done was kiss her, he thought, struggling to put what had happened into perspective. But it wasn't what had happened that bothered him so much, it was what had almost happened. He'd almost lost control of himself. He'd almost surrendered his intellect to his emotions.

He shuddered at the memory of his mindless response to her. He shouldn't have even wanted to kiss her. Not when he knew she thought he was his brother.

But he had been able to stop. He took what comfort he could from the fact. He hadn't been so wrapped up in his own needs that he had taken advantage of Kali. He hadn't gone so far as to make love to her.

A sharp feeling of regret ripped through him, adding to his sense of unreality. He should be glad that he'd been able to stop. So why wasn't he? Why was it that all he felt was a sense of incompleteness?

A sudden gust of icy wind penetrated Hassan's pre-occupation, and he shivered violently. He blinked and looked around, surprised to find that he was standing outside Kali's apartment building in his shirtsleeves. He didn't even remember leaving the building.

He quickly hailed a cruising taxi, ignoring the cabbie's curious looks.

"Here you are, mister." The cabbie pulled up in front of Karim's apartment building ten freezing minutes later.

Now what? Hassan wondered as he rode the elevator up to Karim's apartment.

Nothing had changed, he finally decided. That kiss might have forever destroyed his complacent view of himself as a man whose mind ruled his emotions instead of the other way around. But nothing in the real world had substantially changed.

He still faced the same problem of convincing Kali to break her engagement. Grateful to focus on something that he at least had a hope of accomplishing, he tried to logically assess how his campaign was coming along.

The lecture certainly hadn't produced the results he'd expected, but that was probably because Kali hadn't seen the woman's message as having anything to do with her personally. If that were the case, then what he needed to do was to show Kali how being married to a man from the Middle East would affect her personally. But how…

The Casbah! Hassan suddenly remembered the social club on the Upper East Side that catered to Middle-Eastern expatriates. Conservative Middle-Eastern expa-triates. He'd gone there once with a group from his father's consulate and had found the rigid separation of the sexes both archaic and boring. But a modern Western woman like Kali would probably find it maddening.

Not only that, but his taking her there would be sure to give her doubts about what her future would be like if she went ahead with the wedding. And he could increase her doubts by acting like a Hollywood version of the Sheik of Araby, complete with robes for himself and a chador for her.

It just might be enough to get her to break the engagement.

Hassan tried to ignore the sense of loss he felt at the thought of never seeing Kali again.

It had to be, he reminded himself grimly. He couldn't become involved with a Western woman on any meaningful level, and he didn't think there was any other way but meaningful with someone as special as Kali.

He would take her to the Casbah tomorrow night as soon as she got home from work. The fact that she'd probably be tired would make her all the more susceptible to doubts about him.

He fumbled with the key as he let himself into Karim's apartment. He was so tired all he wanted to do was to fall into bed and sleep until he could see Kali again.

He didn't have the opportunity. A phone call from his father early the next morning led him to spend the entire day trying to trace a shipment of nuclear medical equipment that a California company had shipped, but which had never arrived at the kingdom's new pediatric hospital.

He'd finally managed to track the equipment to a warehouse in Southampton, England, shortly after five.

It took another twenty-five minutes for him to arrange to have it air-lifted to Saad Dev'a on the following day.

As a result it was a mad scramble for him to reach Kali's by six. He buzzed her apartment. When there was no answer, he settled down to wait for her to arrive, trying not to notice the curious stares he was getting from people passing through the lobby.

He was beginning to think that *Gentleman's Quarterly* was right. Clothes really did make the man.

Impatiently he pushed back a fold of his white *kaffiyeh* off his cheek. He hadn't expected to feel so out of place in his robes. Rather as if he'd shown up for a formal reception wearing a bathing suit.

But that was to the good, he tried to tell himself. If he felt this conspicuous wearing his own native costume, then Kali would feel even more ridiculous wearing the chador he'd brought for her. He shifted the package from one hand to the other.

His thoughts became suspended as the lobby door opened and Kali walked in. A wave of longing so intense it threatened to choke him washed over him. He wanted to take her in his arms and kiss away the exhausted look on her pale face.

Kali sighed in pleasure as the warmth of the lobby engulfed her. She was tired, hungry and the headache that had been threatening all afternoon had finally developed into a raging pain.

But her preoccupation with the throbbing between her temples faded as she looked up and saw Hassan.

A hot, burning sensation sparked to life deep in her abdomen as she stared at him. He looked fantastic. Her eyes skimmed over his sparkling white robe to linger on the gleaming golden cords that secured his headpiece.

He looked as if he'd been plucked whole from a Rudolph Valentino movie. All he needed to complete the picture was a white stallion and a band of faithful followers at his back.

She took a deep breath, trying to slow down her thumping heart. She'd ride off into the sunset with him anyday.

"Hi," she said. "I love your robe and that…" She gestured toward his head.

"*Kaffiyeh,*" he automatically supplied. "I like to wear my native garb," he added for good measure.

"I don't blame you." Kali automatically inserted her key into the elevator lock. "I imagine loose robes would be very comfortable in a hot climate."

Especially if he were to wear a minimum of clothing beneath them. Kali felt her mouth dry as she speculatively eyed the flowing garment. What did he have on under it? Her gaze dropped to his feet, and to her disappointment she could see the cuffs of his gray trousers peeking out beneath the hem of the robe.

Hassan surreptitiously studied her as they got into the elevator, trying to judge her reaction to his outfit. He'd expected her to be embarrassed at his unconventional garb, but she didn't seem to be. She seemed to be more curious than anything.

But the lobby had been temporarily deserted when she'd come home. Once they were around other people, she'd probably feel as uncomfortable and out-of-place as he did. Especially when he gave her the chador and told her she had to wear it.

The elevator stopped on the sixth floor and Hassan followed Kali to her apartment, wincing when an elderly lady coming down the hall toward them stopped dead in her tracks and stared at him with her mouth hanging open.

"I'm sorry if I upset your neighbor," he offered, once they were safely inside Kali's apartment.

To his surprise, Kali gave an enchanting gurgle of laughter. "Knowing Mrs. Freidon what probably upset her was that I saw you first. She brings whole new meaning to the term romantic."

Hassan dropped the unpromising subject of Mrs. Freidon's romanticism in favor of pushing his role as a closet male chauvinist.

"We are going out tonight to a club that caters to Middle-Eastern expatriates," he said.

"How nice." Kali made a valiant effort to sound enthusiastic, when what she really wanted to do was to take a hot bath and go to bed. Preferably with Hassan. A shiver of excitement slithered through her as she glanced over her shoulder, and her eyes met the firm line of his lips. Maybe afterward, she consoled herself.

"Let me get a couple of aspirins, and then I'll change," she said, heading toward the kitchen.

Opening the cabinet where she kept her aspirin, she shook out two, considered the fact that she was going to be spending the evening at a nightclub and added a third.

"Don't take more than two aspirin at a time." Hassan's medical training surfaced.

"Don't practice medicine without a license," Kali said and popped all three in her mouth, washing them down with a stale soda which was sitting on the counter.

"But..." Hassan stopped in frustration.

"Besides, I always take three for really bad headaches." She rubbed her slim fingers over her temples, and Hassan felt an urge to comfort her.

Acting on the impulse, he pulled her unresisting body up against him. She felt so absolutely right in his arms.

"Bad day?" he asked, struggling to keep his mind on something other than how she felt and what he'd like to do about it.

"I overslept and was late for my first appointment. It was all downhill from there." She snuggled her face against his neck, relishing the scent and texture.

Hassan gulped as he felt his body begin to react to her closeness. He wasn't sure why, but it seemed as if every time he took her in his arms, he became more susceptible to her.

Stepping back, he forced a brisk note into his voice. "An evening out is just what you need to relax."

"Hmm," Kali murmured, keeping her doubts to herself. She opened the refrigerator, looking for something to snack on.

Pulling out a covered dish, she opened it and tried to identify its contents. She couldn't.

"That smells like it spoiled. Weeks ago." Hassan took it out of her hands and dumped the contents down the garbage disposal.

"I'll buy you dinner at the club," he said.

"I don't think I'll last that long." Kali resumed her rummaging in the refrigerator. "I didn't have time for breakfast and had to fit a very distraught patient into my lunch hour."

"You took three aspirin on an empty stomach!" Hassan didn't have to fake his authoritarian tone. "Have you no sense, woman? You'll wind up with holes in the lining of your stomach!"

"Nonsense." She found a cup of strawberry yogurt and checked the expiration date. It was five weeks ago.

She really did need to find time to go to the grocery store.

"I'll scramble you an egg while you get ready." He took an egg from the holder in the refrigerator door. "Where do you keep your pans?"

Kali didn't bother to tell him she loathed eggs. She was too intrigued with the thought of him actually cooking something for her. His concern, even though she felt he was grossly exaggerating the danger of taking aspirin on an empty stomach, gave her a strange feeling that she couldn't quite identify. She wasn't used to anyone worrying about her except her mother, and her mother expressed worry by nagging.

"The pan," Hassan repeated, and Kali got one out of the cabinet for him.

"If you're going to cook, you really ought to take off that white robe before you spill something on it," she said with the vague hope that once he took it off, he wouldn't want to get dressed again to leave.

Suddenly curious, she leaned a little closer to him, looking for a zipper. "How does it fasten?"

"With Velcro," he said absently as he considered her words. She was right. He should take it off. He felt silly enough wearing it. He'd feel even more ridiculous wearing it with egg splattered on it.

"Velcro?" Kali giggled, and the sound slipped enticingly through his mind.

"Velcro hardly fits the Lawrence of Arabia image you're projecting."

Hassan didn't reply. He was too busy wondering if she liked the Lawrence of Arabia image. Telling himself that it was irrelevant, he tossed his *kaffiyeh* on the table and, ripping open the Velcro fastener, stepped out of the robe.

Kali picked up the *kaffiyeh* and slipped it over her head. It was too big.

Hassan's eyes narrowed at the tantalizing vision she made. Somehow the masculine headpiece emphasized her extreme femininity.

"What do I look like?" Kali pushed it off her face.

Hassan swallowed the urge to tell her just how fantastic she looked and said, "Women don't wear *kaffiyehs.* Women wear chadors. There's one in that package I set on the table beside your front door."

"Really?" Kali looked intrigued.

Taking off his *kaffiyeh,* she dropped it on top of the robe and hurried out into the living room.

Hassan followed.

Kali tore open the package and pulled out what looked like a voluminous, black silk sheet.

"How come you get white and gold, and I just get plain old black?" she complained.

"Custom," he gave the reply he must have heard a million times when he'd been growing up. "Middle-Eastern males don't want their women to wear anything which might draw the masculine eye."

Kali shook the chador out and studied it thoughtfully. "Actually what this might draw is an ambulance if I were dumb enough to try wearing it in a hot climate. If I remember my color theory right, black absorbs light. And your white reflects it."

Hassan shrugged. "Don't blame me. I didn't make up the rules. I'm just a product of my culture."

Instead of looking infuriated or, at the very least, worried by his callous-sounding comment, Kali gave him a slow smile that sent his hormones rocketing into overdrive.

"Let me make sure I've got this straight," she said.

"Your contention is that a person isn't responsible for their behavior if their culture predisposes them to act that way?"

Hassan studied the intoxicating tilt of her lips as he struggled to follow her line of reasoning. It was hopeless. Rational thought didn't stand a chance against the lure of Kali's body.

"Then it's not my fault, either," she said.

Her fault? Hassan wondered, having the unsettling feeling that he'd somehow missed part of the conversation. Weren't they talking about how repressive his culture was?

His thoughts irrevocably fragmented when Kali suddenly launched herself at him. He automatically caught her, gathering her to him.

"What are you doing?" He tried to focus on her actions, instead of how her actions were making him feel.

"I'm applying your principle of disassociation to me. Since I'm only a product of my culture and since my culture is big into freedom of expression and self-gratification…"

She deliberately wiggled against him.

Hassan stared down into her laughing face and was lost. He couldn't think of anything beyond the compulsion to kiss her.

His arms instinctively tightened, and his mouth hungrily sought hers.

Kali made no attempt to even pretend that she didn't welcome his kiss. Her arms slipped up over the smooth material of his suit jacket to clasp his head, imperiously tugging him closer.

She breathed deeply, drawing the scent of him deep into her lungs.

She loved the way he smelled, she thought dreamily.

Clean and sharp, yet with dreamy edges that hinted at the bliss to be found in his lovemaking.

The jarring memory of him all but running from her last night brought her back to reality with a thump, and she forced herself to move away from him while she was still able to act as if their kiss was nothing more than a bit of lighthearted fun.

She ran her tongue over her lower lip as she concentrated on getting her erratic breathing back under control. Her plan was to gently push against the sexual barriers he'd erected and see if they could be breached, she reminded herself. An all-out frontal assault was not part of her plan. At least, not yet.

"Food," Hassan muttered, refocusing with a monumental effort. "You should eat."

Man does not live by bread alone, Kali thought, encouraged by his abstracted expression.

"Good idea," she said. "I'll change while you scramble my egg. Tell me, what does one wear to wherever it is we're going?"

"The Casbah. Just a dress of some kind."

"The Casbah?" Kali giggled. "Now there's a name fraught with all kind of innuendo."

"I go there quite often to relax," Hassan lied. "It reminds me of home."

"Sounds reasonable. I won't be long."

Hassan watched her disappear into her bedroom and fought the urge to follow her. To put off their trip to the Casbah until tomorrow night. They could stay here and watch television and... His vision blurred as in his mind's eye he pictured what else they might do.

He ruthlessly throttled his erotic thoughts. He had no right to make love to her. He wasn't going to marry her. He couldn't marry her. His loyalties had long since been promised elsewhere. Kali had no place in the life he'd so meticulously planned.

Returning to the kitchen, Hassan began to scramble her an egg, his mind on the upcoming evening.

When she was banished to the upper room with the other women, a great many of whom wouldn't even be able to speak English, she'd undoubtedly remember the lecture. Those two events should be enough to set off a whole carillon of alarm bells in her mind.

Thirty-five minutes later their taxi came to a neck-snapping stop in front of the brilliantly lit Casbah. Not looking forward to the next few hours, Hassan paid the cabbie and reluctantly climbed out of the taxi.

Hearing a muffled squeak, he turned around in time to catch Kali as she tumbled into his arms.

"Sorry," she muttered. "I tripped on the hem of this—" she gathered the voluminous chador around her "—walking death trap."

"You'll get used to it." He did his best to sound unconcerned even though the possessive grip he maintained on her arm belied his tone.

Did women ever get used to the chador? he wondered. Was that why the women in his father's kingdom tended to stay at home? Because it was too awkward, not to say dangerous, to venture out in traffic trailing yards of unwieldy material?

Get used to it? Kali examined his words as she followed him across the sidewalk to the garishly painted pink door of the Casbah. Did that mean that Hassan expected her to wear a chador very often? Or did he mean that he wanted her to get used to wearing it, so that when they visited his own country she would be able to wear the outfit without falling flat on her face?

Undoubtedly the latter, she decided, and since the pressures of their jobs would preclude either frequent or extended visits, she could afford to be generous about wearing the chador when they did go.

The door was opened a second after Hassan knocked, and a short, dark man peered out at them.

"Hassan Rashid. I have reservations."

"Of course, sir. Welcome to the Casbah." The man smiled warmly at Hassan. "The floor show will be starting in about twenty minutes and will be repeated again at ten."

The man's gaze skittered over Kali as if he'd just noticed her and was trying to decide if he should acknowledge her or not.

Apparently not, Kali concluded since he addressed his next comment to Hassan.

"There is also entertainment planned for the women upstairs at the same time."

"What kind of entertainment?" Kali asked.

The man ignored her question, and Kali bit back an urge to grab him by his jacket lapels and force him to recognize her as a person.

It doesn't matter, she told herself. It's just a cultural thing. His attitude has nothing to do with you personally.

But even if the man's behavior wasn't directed at her personally, she might very well begin to take it personally in time, she realized with a tremor of unease. Being subjected to such belittling treatment was a lot like being stoned to death with pebbles. None of the individual blows were harmful, but the continual barrage of them finally wore one down. Rather like that woman who'd given the lecture last night had discovered.

Hassan glanced down at Kali, telling himself he should be pleased at her tightly compressed lips. It meant his plan was working. Kali was being forced to face the unbridgeable differences between their cultures.

By the end of the evening she should be ready to break off her engagement. But before she was banished upstairs with the other women, he wanted to make sure she had a good square meal. One slightly scorched scrambled egg wasn't enough to cushion her stomach from the effect of all those aspirin she'd taken.

"We wish to eat first," Hassan told their host.

"Certainly, the woman—"

"Together. I wish to make sure she eats properly." Hassan produced an explanation for his desire to keep Kali close a little longer that the man would understand.

Kali bit back a giggle at the poor man's expression. Clearly he approved of Hassan keeping track of everything she did, but equally clear was his strong desire to hustle her upstairs before her presence somehow contaminated the other men.

"It shall be as you wish, sir," the man finally said. "We have private dining rooms for our guests. If you would follow me?" He turned and headed down a hallway to their right.

Pausing about halfway down the long, narrow hallway, the man pulled aside the deep blue curtain to reveal a small room and gestured them inside.

"If you will be seated, I will send your waiter at once."

Kali looked around the tiny room curiously. There were no table or chairs. Instead, a beautiful red-and-gold Oriental carpet covered the floor and scattered around on it were half a dozen oversize cushions. To sit on?

"We sit on the cushions," Hassan confirmed her guess, "and dinner is placed in front of us."

"I'm game." Kali took the chador, dropped it on the

carpet and then gracefully sank down on a bright red down-filled cushion, which billowed up around her slight figure.

She looked up at Hassan. From her spot on the floor, he appeared enormous in his voluminous white robes. Enormous and eminently desirable. She wanted to put her arms around him and kiss him. To insinuate herself beneath his robes and explore his hard body.

"Normally a woman would never be permitted to eat with a man," Hassan hurried to point out, in case she'd missed the significance of their host's hesitation. It was a fact that had always infuriated his own mother. "They wait until all the men have eaten and then they get the leftovers."

"Ten to one, they've been sampling the food as they prepared it and aren't very hungry by the time the men are served," Kali said.

Hassan's answer was interrupted by the sound of a throat being cleared on the other side of the curtain.

"Come in," Hassan called and the curtain was pulled back to reveal a middle-aged man dressed all in black.

Ignoring Kali, he spoke to Hassan, "I am your waiter, Mustafa. What is your pleasure this evening, sir?"

Hassan conversed with the man in low tones. After the waiter had left, Hassan told Kali, "I ordered a traditional dish for you to try."

"From the looks of this place, I doubt you had much choice," she said dryly. "They don't exactly look to be on the cutting edge of anything but male chauvinism."

"It's tradition."

"You have a lot in common with my mother," Kali said. "She used that argument on my sister and me when we were kids and the family went to Scotland and she wanted us to eat haggis."

"Haggis?" Hassan sat down beside her, even though he knew he should be sitting across from her. When he was near her, he found it hard to remember what he was supposed to be doing. All he could think about was what he wanted to do.

"It's a traditional Scots dish made up of the lungs and heart of a sheep and cooked in its stomach."

Hassan blinked. "That sounds very…"

Kali grinned at him. "Yes, doesn't it. You Arabs certainly don't have a monopoly on indulging in inexplicable behavior and calling it tradition."

The throat clearing sounded again, and Kali turned to the door, curious to see what they'd be served. Eating that scrambled egg had only made her realize just how hungry she really was.

At a word from Hassan, the waiter held back the curtain so that a second man carrying a large shallow bowl and what appeared to Kali to be a metal teapot could enter. He set the bowl down in front of Hassan.

Picking up the teapot, the man waited until Hassan held his hands over the bowl and then he poured a stream of water over them. Hassan dried himself and the man gathered up his equipment and left.

The waiter called to someone out in the hallway and a third man entered carrying a large silver platter filled with steaming food. Placing it in front of Hassan, they all left.

"I take it the hand washing is ceremonial," Kali asked curiously.

"Yes, for males. It's—"

"Tradition," Kali finished. "I'd like to introduce those guys to a few of my ancestors' traditions. The Druids were very into human sacrifice, you know."

Hassan bit back a chuckle at her aggrieved expression.

This wasn't the time to sympathize, he reminded himself. This was the time to emphasize the difference between their cultures.

"You eat with your fingers and only use your right hand," Hassan instructed.

Kali stared down at the platter of food curiously. "That looks like a thin bread on the bottom and rice on top of that. What's the meat and the sauce?"

"Boiled lamb and a seasoned butter sauce. Try some."

Kali obediently broke off a piece of the bread and used it to scoop up some of the rice.

"It's pretty good," she decided, catching a few stray grains of rice with the tip of her tongue.

Hassan watched as she struggled to handle the crisp bread and felt a surge of tenderness at her earnest expression. She was such an open-minded person. Always willing to sample something before she condemned it out of hand. She was someone who could appreciate his background without feeling threatened by it.

But his background was also his future, he reminded himself. Something he couldn't allow himself to forget for a moment.

"There is a skill to eating with your fingers," he began, and the bread he was using as a spoon promptly broke, spilling butter-soaked rice down the front of his robe.

Kali giggled at his annoyed expression. "I know. Do you want me to show you how to do it?"

"Damn," Hassan muttered, ineffectively brushing at the large grease spot.

"Maybe it didn't go through to the other side," Kali said.

Using the comment as an excuse, she pulled the hem of his robe up and stuck her head beneath it.

Hassan's breath caught in his throat as he felt the warmth of her body crowding against him.

"What are you doing?" he asked.

"Checking to see if the stain went all the way through the material. If it hasn't, you can turn your robe inside out."

She moved slightly, and he felt the silky softness of her hair brush against his neck. He tensed as his body began to react to her closeness.

"Not only did that butter sauce soak through your robe, but I think it stained your suit," she said.

Hassan felt her hand slip beneath his jacket and rub enticingly over his chest. The faint pressure of her probing fingers was a goad to his growing response.

She felt so wonderful. So incredibly sexy. So…

The sound of footsteps passing by the curtained door finally penetrated his self-absorption and he made an effort to regain control of the situation.

"Kali, stop that. We're in a public restaurant."

"No, we aren't." She began to rub the palm of her hand over his chest in slow, seductive circles. "We're in a private dining room with a waiter who refuses to even notice me."

"He's going to be hard-pressed not to notice, if he comes back and finds you underneath my robes." Hassan tried to sound disapproving, but it didn't quite come off.

"Do you mean to tell me that his first reaction won't be to assume that there's an innocent explanation for this?" Kali's voice was threaded with a laughter that lured him even deeper into the sensual web she was weaving. She made him feel so alive. As if every second spent in her company was a special moment out of time that was to be cherished and savored because it might never come again.

And it wouldn't, he thought, feeling a wave of incredible loss. Tonight would surely be enough to convince her that she could never marry a man from the Middle East.

Fumbling with the knot of his tie, Kali loosened it to gain access to his skin beneath. Pressing her lips against the base of his throat, she lightly licked the indentation there.

Hassan's arms closed convulsively around her. His breath caught in anticipation as her wandering hand inched downward over his chest.

The sound of a throat being cleared on the other side of the curtain hit Hassan like a shower of icy water.

To his mingled relief and disappointment, Kali also heard the waiter, and she hastily emerged from beneath his robe. It was all he could do not to pull her back into his arms and kiss her.

"'The world is too much with us soon and late,'" she muttered, brushing her hair out of her face. Not that it mattered because the waiter ignored her.

"Is there anything else you require, sir?" the waiter asked.

"No," Hassan said, resisting the urge to prolong dinner with another course. It was time to get on with his plan.

"Very good, sir. I shall wait outside to escort—" the waiter glanced at Kali as if trying to decide how to refer to her and settled on "—your, er, companion upstairs to the women's area."

He stepped outside, and Kali turned to Hassan. "But we haven't had dessert!" Her eyes glittered with suppressed laughter and a tantalizing promise that sent an answering rush of emotion through Hassan, which he struggled to keep hidden.

"You can have something with the women. Order anything you want," he said.

"I sincerely doubt that what I want is on the menu."

"Behave yourself!" Hassan did his best to sound straitlaced.

"I think that should be my line considering where we are," Kali said slowly as she suddenly wondered for the first time just what constituted male entertainment in a place like this.

Other women? A burning flash of stark jealousy poured through her that she did her best to ignore. She trusted Hassan, she told herself as she draped the chador around herself. What she didn't trust were the other inmates in this asylum for rampant chauvinism.

"You'll enjoy yourself with the other women," Hassan said, knowing that he wouldn't be enjoying himself with the men. He didn't want to spend his evening socializing with them. He wanted to spend it with Kali.

Duty, he dredged the cold, comfortless word out of the depths of his soul. He had a duty to perform.

Getting to his feet, Hassan walked with Kali out of the tiny dining alcove and watched as the waiter escorted her to the stairs that led to the women's room on the second floor. Not even the bulky chador could hide the grace of her fluid movements.

He continued to watch until she disappeared through a doorway at the top of the stairs and then he reluctantly turned and headed toward the large central room where the men were congregated.

The floor show had already started, and he sat down at an empty table near the back of the room.

Idly he watched the belly dancer's gyrations, mentally applauding the woman's skill. She appeared to be an expert at the art.

"Man, wouldn't I like to have that one to warm my bed," the man at the table next to Hassan said to him.

Hassan looked back at the dancer, taking in her long, black hair, which brushed over the tips of her full, barely covered breasts. Curiously he probed his reaction to the sight and discovered a vast indifference. He might as well have been looking at someone's eighty-year-old grandmother.

The dancer was simply too…too much, he thought, as an image of Kali's much slighter body filled his mind, and his body hardened almost painfully at the thought.

He wanted Kali and no one else, he realized. His sense of dismay set the final cap on what was turning out to be a miserable evening.

But if he was miserable, then Kali should not only be equally miserable, but bored out of her mind. He tried to draw what comfort he could from the situation.

He was wrong. Boredom was the furthest thing from Kali's mind as she stared in wide-eyed fascination at the controlled movements of the woman on the tiny raised dais at the front of the room.

"Belly dancing is an art form," one of the women beside Kali said, noticing her interest. "And you can take off your chador here. In fact, you'd better before you faint from the heat."

Kali slipped out of the enveloping material, her eyes never leaving the woman's gyrations. "I don't know about an art form, but I'd have sworn you couldn't make your stomach muscles do that."

"It takes a lot of practice," the woman said. "I took

lessons for a couple of years when my husband was stationed in Egypt, but then he was sent to Europe and I dropped out.''

"Does she give lessons?" Kali asked as an idea began to form in her mind. Hassan wanted her to become acquainted with his culture, and she couldn't think of a more intriguing place to start than belly dancing. It was one of the most erotic things she'd ever seen. The absolutely perfect tool for seduction.

"I don't know, but I'd be glad to introduce you, and you can ask. I do know you can buy one of those outfits like the one she's wearing here at the club if you like."

"Oh, I'd like," Kali said. But more important, how would Hassan like it? She tingled with excitement. Kali could hardly wait to get home and find out.

Seven

The crowd of women coming down the stairs of the Casbah parted slightly, and Hassan caught a glimpse of Kali's sparkling brown eyes, which was all that was visible of her beneath the concealing chador she wore. Her head was bent toward a middle-aged woman who was saying something that Kali appeared to find fascinating.

Could the woman be telling her about the insurmountable problems a Western women would face if she tried to live in the Middle East? Hassan wondered.

The sudden gust of muffled laughter that came from the group seemed to dispute the idea, and Hassan felt a surge of annoyance at their evident good humor. He certainly hadn't found anything even remotely funny about the evening he'd just passed. He had been alternately bored and infuriated by his companions' narrow-minded outlook on life. But despite his intense frustration, he'd forced himself to stay until closing because he'd assumed that Kali was having an equally miserable time. And yet when the closing bell had brought the women down from the second floor, Kali had been at the center of an animated crowd.

Hassan felt distinctly annoyed at the unfairness of it all. He didn't understand what a vibrant, modern career woman like Kali could possibly have found to talk about with a group of women who had no interest beyond their own homes. She should have had no point of contact with them at all, and yet she seemed to be enjoying their company. Or could it be that she was hiding her frustrations beneath a polite social mask? He already knew she was a kind person. Too kind to let her companions know that she found them boring. Maybe that was it. Maybe his plan had worked after all.

Impatient to leave so that he could find out, Hassan waved at Kali, trying to catch her attention. The woman next to Kali pointed toward Hassan.

Kali turned and saw him, said something to the middle-aged woman she'd been talking to and then grinned.

Her smile sliced through all the petty frustrations of Hassan's evening like the proverbial hot knife through butter. It also increased his desire for her a hundredfold. He shifted uncomfortably as his body began to react to her.

He could control his growing need for her, he assured himself. He wasn't some savage at the mercy of his emotions. He was an educated man who'd never had any trouble in the past keeping his impulses under control.

But then, when his eyes lingered on the graceful movement of Kali's body as she made her way through the crowd toward him, he knew he'd never met anyone quite like Kali.

"Hi," she said when she finally reached him.

"How was your evening?" Hassan probed.

"Your culture has some fascinating aspects to it."
Kali instinctively hugged the brown-paper-wrapped
package she was carrying. "There was a woman there
named Fatima who gave a demonstration of belly dancing. I never realized before that it was an aerobic exercise."

Hassan hastily chopped off the intoxicating images
that flooded his mind at the twin thoughts of Kali and
belly dancing together. Intense frustration made his
voice curt.

"Belly dancing isn't from my culture." He led her
over to the doorman who was busily hailing cabs for the
departing patrons. "I think it's Egyptian. So there's no
reason for you to bother with it."

"That argument won't hold water in today's world,"
Kali said. "You aren't Western, but you wear Western
suits both to work and beneath your robes. You aren't
French, but you take advantage of Pasteur's theories of
vaccines to immunize yourself against all kinds of nasty
little bugs. And you certainly use Western technology in
every aspect of your life. At the risk of sounding trite,
the world is a very small place these days. People tend
to pick and choose what they want from a whole smor-
gasbord of cultures."

The doorman gestured them toward the next taxi, and
in the bustle of getting in, Hassan was spared the necessity of answering. Which was a good thing, he admitted, because he didn't have an answer. Even though
he felt her argument was simplistic, there was a great
deal of truth to it. Especially where he was concerned.
He really was a hybrid—a man whose roots were in the
Middle East, but whose upbringing and life-style had a
decided Western slant to it.

The result was that he didn't really belong to either culture. A feeling of loneliness pressed down on him. Not in the West, where his mother had chosen to live her life, and not in the Middle East, where duty had trapped his father. And even worse, there was no one in the whole world who understood how adrift he felt, and there never would be.

The knowledge of just how isolated he would always be made him feel faintly frantic. He grimly fought back the feeling that he was caught in quicksand and sinking.

"Four-fifty!" The impatience in the taxi driver's voice told Hassan that that probably wasn't the first time he'd said it.

Hassan hurriedly fumbled beneath his robes to find his wallet and paid the man, while Kali, still clutching her package, climbed out of the cab.

"What did you buy?" he asked as he followed Kali into her apartment building. "Have they started selling takeout at the Casbah?"

"There's food for the body and food for the soul," Kali said. She could hardly wait to get Hassan upstairs and try out her fledgling belly dancing skills on him.

"It's too big to be a Koran, which is all the food the soul needs!" he snapped. He felt so miserable that he wanted everyone around him to be miserable, too. Still, he knew it wasn't Kali's fault that he was trapped in a way of life that suddenly felt several sizes too small.

Snap out of it! he ordered himself, making a valiant effort to control his bad mood. He couldn't change his own fate. It was far too late for that, but he could ensure that Kali escaped emotionally unscathed from her encounter with the Rashid family.

Kali automatically pushed the button for the sixth floor as she tried to make sense of Hassan's mood. He didn't seem so much preoccupied as grumpy and out of sorts. Or maybe what he was feeling was frustration? As in sexual frustration?

A sizzling spark of excitement tore through her.

Hassan was an intriguing mixture of two very different cultures, and it was becoming increasingly obvious to her that at times the two halves did not always mesh well. Could his Western side want to make love to her while his Middle-Eastern side was telling him that it was wrong until after they were married?

It was possible. It was also possible that sex had nothing whatsoever to do with his strange mood. Simply because her every second thought was of making love to him didn't mean that he was thinking along similar lines.

She shot a quick glance over her shoulder at him as the elevator stopped and they got off. The alluring sight of his dark features, outlined by the pristine white of his *kaffiyeh* quickened her heart beat.

Hurriedly she unlocked her door, determined to risk seducing him. He'd given her the perfect opening. She glanced down at the package she was carrying. He'd been the one to take her to the Casbah.

The worst thing to happen would be that he'd claim he had a headache and leave. A nervous giggle escaped her at the thought.

"What's the matter?" Hassan asked.

"Um, nothing." Kali took a deep breath, trying to calm her jittery nerves.

"Why don't you get yourself a drink, and I'll be right back," Kali said, leaving to change into her costume.

"But—" Hassan began only to find that he was talking to her disappearing back.

"Hell!" he muttered and went to run his fingers

through his hair only to encounter the thick, white material of his *kaffiyeh*.

"Double hell!" In frustration he yanked it off and flung it on the couch. The robe followed. He refused to go home looking like a refugee from a Halloween party. Especially since there was no need. Kali wouldn't be going home with him.

The knowledge sent a burst of self-pity through him that disgusted him. He knew he had no reason to feel sorry for himself. He was healthy; he had a profession he loved, even if he wasn't going to be able to practice it much longer; and more money than he could ever spend. Lots of people would sell their souls to trade places with him. The knowledge left him cold.

"Close your eyes." Kali's voice came from behind him. He obediently closed his eyes, focusing on the sound of her voice to keep his unhappy thoughts at bay.

There was a rustle of movement as she walked around him and then she said, "Okay, you can open them now."

Hassan opened his eyes and then immediately closed them again, unable to believe he was seeing what he thought he was seeing. He felt disoriented. As if he'd somehow been catapulted into the fantasy he'd indulged in during the floor show at the Casbah.

Cautiously he opened his eyes again. Nothing had changed. Kali was still wearing a provocative costume consisting of long filmy blue scarves and glittering silver sequins.

His eyes widened as she moved toward him, and the scarves parted to show the firm skin of her slender thighs. All he could think of was a story from his school days about a Greek named Tantalus, who, as a punishment for something or other, had had to stand in water but hadn't been able to reach it to quench his thirst. Just as he couldn't slake his raging thirst for Kali.

Kali was elated by the glitter in Hassan's eyes. Her outfit had certainly affected him on some level. Now if she could just get him thinking like a Westerner....

"Isn't this outfit spectacular?" She turned around to give him the full benefit of it. "I bought it from the woman who gave the belly dancing demonstration."

Kali slowly raised her arms mimicking Fatima's dancing and then lowered them past her breasts as if to bring them to his attention.

"Fatima said that she gives lessons at the Y. I think it would be great exercise, don't you?" She lowered her voice to a beguiling whisper.

It didn't make any sense, Hassan thought in confusion. Kali didn't have a fraction of the skill of the performer he'd watched earlier at the Casbah. Yet that woman had left him cold, while just the sight of Kali wearing those exotic bits and pieces of blue stuff set the blood pounding so hard in his head he couldn't think straight.

"Belly dancing raises the heart rate very satisfactorily," she murmured as she leaned toward him.

"Heart rate?" he repeated distractedly as she began to move her hips in an undulating movement. The long, silk scarves attached to the waist of the bikini bottom floated back and forth, revealing and then concealing her legs.

"Oh, yes. Belly dancing is marvelous for your heart." The husky whisper of her voice rasped over his nerve endings, increasing his sense of edginess. He felt as if he were standing on the edge of a precipice and the slightest movement would send him plunging into an abyss of sexual desire that would wholly consume him.

Leaning toward him, Kali grabbed his tie and slowly loosened the knot.

He could feel the material slide around his neck as she tugged it free. Slowly she pulled it between her fingers as if she were learning its texture by heart. Hassan watched it slip so suggestively over her flesh that he began wishing she would touch him like that.

Seeming to lose interest in his tie, Kali tossed it behind her. Hassan had no idea where it landed. His attention was focused on the movement of her scantily covered breasts as she threw it.

His breath caught in his throat as her body began to sway as if in response to music only she could hear. She jerked her hips back and the scarves flipped at him.

Instinctively he grabbed for one, and she laughingly retreated, keeping just out of reach even though she was encouraged by his reaction. On some level Hassan certainly wanted her. How much and what he was willing to do about it remained to be seen.

"My dear sir," Kali leaned toward him and inhaled, forcing her breasts half out of their brief covering. "You mustn't touch. This isn't interactive entertainment. I'm giving a demonstration."

Of what? Hassan wondered. How much frustration the human male could take before he went stark raving mad?

"About heart rate, remember," she said. She swayed forward to within inches of him.

Hassan could feel her perfume teasing his nostrils, luring him ever deeper into an all-enveloping miasma of sexual desire. He gulped in great lungfuls of air in a vain attempt to control his increasingly erratic breathing.

His muscles began to twitch beneath his left eye as she reached out and started to unbutton his shirt. When she had it open, she tugged it free from his pants and then pressed the palm of her hand flat on his bare chest.

Reaction shot through him like a tidal wave, tumbling his thoughts over and over until they were hopelessly scrambled.

"See." Her satisfied voice echoed in his ears. "I told you belly dancing raised the heart rate."

Her words made no sense to him. Nothing did but the feel of her hands on his chest and the warmth of her scantily clad body standing so bewitchingly close to him.

He trembled as she flexed her fingers. The sensuous movement fogged his thoughts, making it hard for him to think clearly. The very intensity of his reaction set alarm bells ringing deep in his mind, but they were muted. As if he heard them from a great distance.

It was all right, he told himself. He could control his desire. He had last night. Last night he'd kissed her and then left. He could do the same thing tonight. He was in control of the situation. And of himself.

"What are you doing?" The question was torn out of him as Kali inched her fingers around his rib cage.

"I'm trying to tickle you, and finding it hard going!"

"I'm not ticklish, but if you thought of the idea in the first place then it must be because you are."

"Hassan! Don't you dare!" Reacting instinctively to the devilish light that suddenly sparked to life in his eyes, Kali jerked sideways. The top of her costume caught on the button of his shirt cuff, coming undone.

Hassan gulped at the unexpected sight of her naked breasts so tantalizingly close to him. Slowly, hesitantly, almost afraid to touch her for fear the vision was just a figment of his fevered imagination, he cupped her breasts with fingers that trembled beneath the force of his longing.

Her satiny skin felt hot. Burningly hot as if she shared the excitement tormenting him. His breath caught in his throat as his thumbs brushed her rose-colored nipples, and they hardened against his palm. He could feel her heart pounding against his palm. The throbbing beat fed his growing excitement, sucking him deeper and deeper into the whirlpool of his passion.

Just a kiss, he told himself. One kiss and then he'd go home. He could handle it. He wasn't some callow youth to lose control just because he had a beautiful woman in his arms.

Lowering his head, Hassan pressed his mouth against the warm velvety slope of one breast, breathing in the erotic scent that clung to her. It was stronger this close. And infinitely more alluring.

Tentatively his tongue darted out to lick at her nipple, and the strength of the hunger gripping him made quick work of his inhibitions. Without giving it a conscious thought, he caught at her turgid nipple and suckled, trembling when Kali moaned in reaction.

She liked him to touch her, he realized, and the knowledge was like pouring gasoline on a blazing fire. Suddenly the need to feel her breasts against his bare chest overwhelmed every other rational consideration, and he hurriedly shrugged out of his shirt, letting it fall to the floor.

His arms closed around her. He pulled her to him, binding her body against him as if he would absorb her into his very being.

He could see a pulse pounding at the base of her neck. Fascinated, he pressed his lips to the spot, allowing the throbbing rhythm to seep into his muddled senses.

Kali arched her lower body against his growing hardness, and her provocative movement unraveled the last few threads of his self-control.

Hassan felt as if he had somehow slipped over the edge of a mountain and was careering downhill, hopelessly out of control. And the worst part was he didn't care. He didn't care about anything except that the feeling not stop.

His mouth closed over hers with a consuming hunger he made no attempt to hide. He needed the contact. Needed to feed on her sweetness to maintain his fast-slipping sanity.

"Yes," he muttered indistinctly as he felt her fumbling with the zipper on his pants. He shifted slightly to help her and then awkwardly kicked them off, gasping when her slender fingers closed along the hot, hard length of him.

His whole being suddenly became focused on the driving need to make her his. To get as close to her as it was possible for a man to get to a woman.

Scooping her up in his arms, he carried her over to the couch and placed her on the soft cushions. The rights and wrongs of what he was doing had no meaning to him at the moment. All that mattered was Kali and how much he wanted to be a part of her.

Using his knee, he nudged her legs apart and, pushing her scanty costume aside, positioned himself and he surged into her.

Intense pleasure at the feel of her hot body surrounding him engulfed him. Sensation poured along his nerves, seeming to lift him up to the very heavens before hurtling him back down to earth in a blaze of joy so great he momentarily lost contact with the real world.

When he came to his senses again it was to find Kali shivering in his arms deep into the throes of her own climax. His arms tightened protectively, wishing he could stretch this magical moment into infinity.

"Thank you," he muttered against her neck, and promptly plummeted into a deep sleep with her still tightly grasped in his arms.

Hassan muttered, protesting the ray of sunlight that nudged him toward full consciousness. He didn't want to wake up. He was having the most delightful dream. He was in paradise, and Kali was his own personal houri. Her delectable body was covered with an assortment of bright red scarves, which kept separating provocatively as she danced. Her arms were held out to him in a welcome as old as time itself.

He moved his head sideways as the discomfort from the sunlight became an actual pain. Reluctantly he opened his eyes and found himself inches from her.

Dreamily he stared at her sleep-relaxed face, his eyes lingering on the thickness of her dark eyelashes lying on her pale cheeks. They looked so enticing. He wanted to kiss them. To explore their texture with his lips.

His eyes drifted lower, down to her soft mouth, and his breath shortened with longing. He wanted to rain kisses over her face. And after he'd done that, he would turn his attention to her body. Last night had been...

Stupid! Incredibly stupid. Full awareness brought with it a wave of guilt so strong it totally extinguished his ardor.

What had he done! How could he have lost control so much as to have made love to her?

A surge of self-disgust rolled through him making him feel faintly nauseous. Kali had thought she had been making love to the man she was going to marry. And he'd taken advantage of her trust to indulge his own lust. What kind of self-indulgent jerk was he?

One who had no self-control where Kali was concerned—the answer was obvious. What wasn't so obvious was what he was supposed to do now.

Hassan took a deep breath trying to think, but he couldn't seem to pull his thoughts together.

The heat from her warm body—her warm, naked body—on the couch next to him destroyed any hope he might have had of rational thought. All he could do was feel. And react to that feeling. He winced as he felt his body hardening.

He had to get away. The thought surfaced through the maelstrom of his growing passion. He had to distance himself from Kali before he compounded his sin by repeating it.

Bracing his uncooperative muscles, he inched off the couch, trying not to waken her. He froze when she muttered at the loss of his warmth, and it was all he could do not to soothe her protest with his lips.

A cold sweat dampened his forehead as his guilt fought with his desire. Finally guilt gained the upper hand, and he was able to turn away.

He needed to get dressed, he thought distractedly, looking around for the clothes he'd been wearing. They were scattered haphazardly on the floor.

Being careful not to look at Kali for fear that his resolve would break and he wouldn't be able to go, Hassan scrambled into his clothes and stealthily left the apartment, feeling like a criminal escaping the scene of a crime.

And in a moral sense he had committed a crime, he castigated himself. He'd made love to Kali under completely false pretenses. The fact that he hadn't intentionally set out to do it didn't excuse his behavior. He'd still done it. He could have stopped himself last night. He could even have kissed her a few times and then gone home like an honorable man would have done.

No. He faced the unpalatable fact. He couldn't have stopped himself. The only thing that could have stopped him from making love to Kali would have been if she herself had said no. He hadn't had the strength to do it on his own. He'd wanted her far too much.

Hassan pushed back his rumpled hair in confusion. He didn't understand his mindless reaction to Kali. He'd never lost control like that before.

Why he'd done it didn't matter, he told himself. What mattered was what he was going to do about it.

The elevator stopped on the ground floor, and Hassan strode across the lobby, not even noticing the young woman by the front door who eyed his wrinkled suit and unshaven face speculatively.

Hassan hailed a cruising taxi and gave the man Karim's address.

What was he supposed to do now? The question ricocheted through Hassan's mind, causing pinpricks of pain. How was he going to tell Kali that she'd made love to the wrong man?

He couldn't, Hassan realized. Telling her what he'd done would only make her feel as bad as he already did. She might even begin to doubt her own ability to judge people, and that would be a disaster in her line of work.

No, relieving his conscience by confessing was out. His only real option was to keep his mouth shut and proceed with his plan to get her to break the engagement herself. That way she need never know.

"Here we are." The taxi driver pulled up in front of Karim's apartment building.

Hassan distractedly handed him a twenty, told him to keep the change and climbed out of the cab.

He rode the elevator up to Karim's apartment, trying to ignore his growing sense of loss at the necessity of irrevocably alienating Kali.

He had to do it, he clung desperately to the thought. He was committed to returning to Saad Dev'a. He wasn't a free agent. He had to convince Kali to break her engagement. But how?

The lecture hadn't worked. Probably because she hadn't felt that what the woman was saying related to her personally. And the Casbah hadn't worked because she'd gotten sidetracked with the belly dancing. He gulped as his body instantly reacted to the memory of her body moving behind the filmy scarves. She wasn't the only one who'd gotten sidetracked by belly dancing.

So what else could he do to make her see just how restrictive the life-style of a Middle-Eastern woman was?

Faisal Sharif! Hassan suddenly remembered a friend of his father's who was not only aggressively conservative, but compulsively gregarious. He owned a ski lodge about two hours north of the city, and he virtually held open house for his fellow countrymen on the weekends. He'd long ago issued a standing invitation to Hassan to visit.

He could take Kali to Faisal's after she got off work this evening, and this time there wouldn't be any entertainment planned for the women that would distract her. It would never occur to Faisal to even acknowledge his female guests, let alone provide for their amusement. Surely after a weekend of her host and his male guests treating her and the other women as if they were third-class citizens, and not too bright ones at that, Kali would realize that a marriage between them could never work.

At least, he sure hoped she came to that conclusion, because he wasn't sure what he was going to do if she didn't. Faisal Sharif was his last idea. If it didn't work, he'd have no choice left but the truth. His soul cringed at the thought of what she would think of his duplicity.

A ringing sound bludgeoned Kali from sleep, and she automatically reached out to turn off the alarm clock only to encounter nothing but air beneath her groping fingers. Confused, she opened her eyes and found that she was lying on the couch instead of on her bed.

Why was she… Hassan! Memory flooded her and her gaze swept the room looking for him. To her disappointment he wasn't there.

After they were married she was going to have to convince him to wake her when he got up. A warmth at the idea of what they could do when he did surged through her only to be extinguished by yet another ring.

The phone! She finally identified the sound and, scrambling off the couch, answered it.

"Hello," she said.

"Kali, did I get you out of bed?"

Kali frowned as she recognized Hassan's voice. Where was he? Clearly not still in the apartment. So why had he left only to call her? And, more important, why wasn't she reacting to the sound of his voice? She felt none of the anticipation and suppressed excitement she normally did.

Unconsciously she closed her eyes, and an image of Hassan's taut features as he'd bent over her last night filled her mind. Her heart began to pound with slow, heavy thuds as she remembered the bright glow of sexual desire that had lit his black eyes.

Kali drew a shaky breath and opened her eyes. The

feelings rioting through her faded away into nothingness as the sound of Hassan's voice echoed meaninglessly in her ears. It made no sense. How could she fall into an agony of longing merely by closing her eyes and remembering their lovemaking and yet the actual sound of his voice envoked no response at all?

Almost desperately Kali focused on Hassan's words, probing deep within herself for a reaction. For a spark of desire, no matter how small. She found nothing.

She shook her head, trying to tell herself that it was just because she wasn't quite awake yet.

"I did get you out of bed, didn't I?" he said ruefully. "I keep forgetting that Australia is halfway around the world."

Thoroughly confused, Kali rubbed her forehead, trying to think. A task that became impossible at his next words.

"I know Hassan told you about my marrying Felicity, but I wanted to call you myself and tell you how happy I am."

Hassan told me? What was he talking about? Wasn't Hassan his family's nickname for Karim? And who is Felicity? Kali's sense of disorientation grew.

"So how did you like my staid twin?"

Twin! The word sliced through Kali's confusion, suddenly bringing her earlier doubts about Hassan into appalling focus. She stared down at her hand, surprised to find it shaking.

"Kali? Are you all right?"

No. Kali bit back an urge to burst into self-pitying tears. She wasn't all right. In fact, she had the disheartening feeling that she wasn't ever going to be all right again.

"I'm just not fully awake." Kali scrambled to sound

normal. "Tell me about your Felicity." She tossed out a red herring, which Karim eagerly grabbed.

He launched into a monologue about the unknown Felicity's multiple charms, which made her sound like a cross between Helen of Troy and Joan of Arc.

Five minutes later Kali was finally able to hang up without Karim realizing that she was getting rid of him. Or just how upset she really was.

She should hate Hassan for what he'd done, she thought in despair. She should, but she didn't. She didn't hate him because she loved him. The realization struck her with the force of a blow, and Kali closed her eyes in instant negation of her appalling discovery.

She didn't want to be in love. Not with Hassan. Not with anyone. Being in love left you open to pain and betrayal.

And as if falling in love weren't bad enough, how could she have fallen in love with a man who was pretending to be someone else? She had no idea.

Nor did she understand why Hassan would have done such a cruel thing. He wasn't a cruel man. Quite the contrary. He was a very compassionate man. She remembered his reaction to the man injured in the car accident. Why would a compassionate man behave so out of character?

A cold tendril of horror slithered down her spine as she suddenly remembered the first thing she'd said to him when he'd come to her apartment last Saturday. That she wanted to see him because she needed him to go to her parents' and lend her moral support for Eddie's christening.

Could Hassan have come to the apartment with the intention of telling her that Karim had married someone else and then not done it because he'd felt sorry for her?

The coldness spread, encircling her chest and playing havoc with her breathing.

Kali began to pace, unable to sit still under the humiliating thought. She didn't even want to consider that what Hassan felt for her was pity, yet common sense told her it was a distinct possibility.

But there had to be more to his feelings for her than pity, she argued with herself. Because if there wasn't why hadn't he told her once the christening was over?

Uncertainly she gnawed on her bottom lip. Why had he continued the charade? Why had he carried it to the extreme of making love to her?

Kali stared at the far wall, trying to remember how he'd reacted to their lovemaking. She couldn't. Not precisely. Their lovemaking had been a confusing jumble of heat and excitement and pleasure, and she found it impossible to sort out the experience. The only thing she was sure of was that if Hassan had been faking his reaction to her, he was the greatest actor since the legendary Edmund Kean.

Kali paced across the floor as she tried to decide what she should do. Confront him and demand an explanation?

No! She instinctively rejected the idea. If she did that, Hassan would probably apologize and disappear from her life forever.

A dark, clammy cloud of fear oozed through her, making her feel faint. She couldn't risk that. The thought of never seeing Hassan again, of never hearing his deep chuckle or seeing the way his eyes twinkled when he was amused—

Kali gulped. It didn't bear thinking about. And she didn't have to think about it, she assured herself. At least, not yet she didn't. As long as Hassan didn't know that she knew who he was, she had some time. Time to try to get him to fall in love with her. But did she have enough time?

And even more problematic was the question of how was she supposed to accomplish it. She didn't have a clue. All she knew for certain was that she had to try, because she didn't know how she could live the rest of her life without him.

Eight

Kali froze as the call button from the lobby buzzed, knowing it had to be Hassan. The message he'd left with her office receptionist that morning had said that he'd pick her up at six to take her away for a weekend of skiing. And it was five minutes to six now.

Nervously she pushed the button to allow him on the elevator. She both dreaded and craved seeing him again—a mixture of emotions that made for a very unsettled frame of mind.

Kali sighed. *Unsettled* didn't begin to describe how confused she felt. And to make matters worse, despite spending every free second of her frantic workday figuring out how to get the man of her dreams to fall in love with her, she still hadn't come up with one single, solid idea.

The doorbell chimed, and she opened it.

"Kali?" Hassan's velvety voice flowed across her nerve endings, increasing her agitation. "You ready?"

"Ready?" she repeated as she studied his sharply chiseled features, searching for a clue to his mood, to his feelings toward her. There was nothing to be read in his face.

"To go skiing," he said, staring down into her pale face. She looked exhausted, Hassan thought. He wanted to take her into his arms and comfort her. But he knew that in the end she'd find it cold comfort. He couldn't offer her anything except the most fleeting emotional involvement, and Kali deserved better than that. She deserved the best there was.

Which was what this weekend was all about, he reminded himself. To free her from her engagement in a way that left her pride and emotions still intact, so that she would be able to find someone else. Someone who would appreciate her unique qualities.

A surge of some dark emotion welled up in him at the thought of Kali in another man's arms. Grimly he beat his reaction back, knowing he had no right to feel possessive of her.

Kali felt a slight easing of her tension at his prosaic words. Apparently Hassan was going to ignore the fact that they'd made love. Which meant that she wasn't going to have to deal with the emotionally charged issue now. She'd have time to build her defenses so that when they did talk about it, hopefully she could respond as a rational adult.

And it would seem Karim hadn't called him, as she'd half feared he would. Hassan didn't know that she knew about his impersonation. She had time to put into action her plan to make him fall in love with her. Just as soon as she could figure out what it was.

"Kali? Are you all right?"

"I'm just a little tired."

Unable to resist her driving need to touch him, Kali leaned against his chest. Encouraged by the way his arms automatically encircled her, she snuggled closer. She rubbed her cheek against the sleek material of his suit jacket, savoring the contact all the more because she didn't know how many more times she would be in his arms.

She hurriedly banished the thought. Her chances of getting Hassan to fall in love with her weren't high to begin with. If she started dwelling on worst-case scenarios, she'd lose what little chance she did have.

Hassan rubbed his cheek over her soft, silky hair, breathing in the intensely feminine scent of it. She smelled like the flowers of an English spring garden.

A distracting image of Kali standing on a verdant green lawn wearing a chain of daisies around her neck and nothing else popped into his mind.

The plan, he hauled his imagination up short. *Remember what has to be.*

"You'll feel better once you've had some exercise," Hassan said.

"I've never bought into that theory. Besides, I can't ski," Kali murmured.

Her warm breath wafted across his neck, tightening his skin.

Hassan glanced down at her, his eyes lingering on the soft pink of her lips.

All day long he'd speculated on her possible reactions to their having made love. He'd pictured scenarios ranging from her throwing her arms around him and telling him that his lovemaking was fantastic to her slamming the door in his face and telling him he was an unprincipled jerk as well as a total loss as a lover.

He found it distinctly anticlimactic that she was treating him in the same friendly manner that she always had. Her acting as though they had never made love both annoyed and relieved him, leaving him feeling frustrated and confused. It wasn't like him to swing from one emotional extreme to another, yet somehow around Kali mood swings seemed to be the norm.

He felt her take a deep breath, and her breasts pushed into his chest. He knew that if he were to turn his head just slightly, he could kiss her.

Action immediately followed the thought. His mouth brushed hers, and a cascade of sparks poured through him, lighting tiny fires the entire length of his body. Fires that became a raging conflagration when she wrapped her arms around his torso and pressed herself against him.

The plan. He grabbed desperately at his chosen role of chauvinistic male, using it to pull himself out of the maelstrom of sexual desire in which he was slowly drowning.

"Why can't you ski?" He latched on to the last thing she'd said.

"I grew up on Long Island, and it's kind of flat."

"I'll teach you. You can have your first lesson tonight."

That wasn't what she wanted a lesson in, Kali thought ruefully. But they couldn't ski all night. Sooner or later they'd have to go inside, and then she'd have a go at doing what she wanted to do. She held down the rising tide of excitement.

Hassan saw her suitcase sitting beside the door and,

picking it up, said, "Did you remember to pack your chador?"

Kali blinked in surprise. "To go skiing? Unless you view skiing as some kind of suicide pact, I doubt it would work very well."

"Not for the skiing. For when we aren't on the slopes. We're visiting the estate of a friend of my father's, Faisal Sharif, and he's rather conservative."

Kali considered Hassan's description of the unknown Faisal as she retrieved the chador from the chair where she'd tossed it the night before and stuffed it into her purse. Being conservative covered a lot of ground. Some aspects of which she didn't even want to think about. Nor did she know how Faisal's politics might affect her own plans. About the only thing she was sure of was that she could have done without the added complication.

Once they were on the highway heading out of the city, Kali decided to try to find out a little more about Faisal.

"Tell me about our host," she said.

"I did. He's conservative."

"Which means exactly what?" she persisted.

"It means that Faisal thinks that women should be neither seen nor heard."

Kali felt a flare of excitement. She was more than willing to spend the weekend closeted with Hassan away from anyone else's eyes.

Her excitement faded as reality reared its ugly head. If Faisal was conservative in the same way those men at the Casbah had been, it would likely mean that the men would spend their time together and the women would, too. Just not in the same place. Which would throw a distinct monkey wrench into her plans.

"He's a friend of my father's," Hassan added just in case she hadn't caught the fact that his family had ties with Faisal.

"With antiquated ideas like that, I didn't think he was a friend of yours."

"I wouldn't want to offend him," Hassan offered.

"I know what you mean. I have a pair of great-aunts who think that the decline of modern civilization is caused by women wearing pants and makeup. Other than that, they're absolute darlings. So every time they visit, I wear a dress and wander around without any makeup, looking like a ghost."

Hassan competently passed a slow-moving double-trailer rig as he tried to decide whether to say anything more about Faisal or to let the matter drop for now.

"Why don't you take a nap so you'll be fresh when we get there," Hassan said instead, worried by her continued paleness. He couldn't cosset her the way he wanted to, but at least he could let her rest before he subjected her to a skiing lesson.

A sense of discouragement at his seeming indifference to her company seemed to press Kali down into the brown leather seat, and she shifted slightly, trying to dislodge the feeling. She couldn't afford to get discouraged. Anything was possible, she assured herself. Maybe not probable, but definitely possible.

She closed her eyes, the better to concentrate on her nebulous plans, and promptly fell asleep.

A sudden bump caused by the Mercedes's right front tire hitting a huge pothole threw Kali against her seat belt, and she opened her eyes, blinking. She turned her head, instinctively relaxing when she saw Hassan.

Skiing. Her memory supplied the details. She was going skiing with Hassan. Her eyes lingered on his fingers, which were gripping the steering wheel, and she felt her stomach twist with longing as she remembered the feel of those fingers moving over her body last night.

"You awake?" To Kali's ears, Hassan's voice sounded preoccupied.

"Uh-huh." She glanced at the dashboard clock, surprised to find that she'd been asleep for almost two hours.

"You should have woken me," she said. "I could have helped with the driving."

About to assure her that he liked driving, he suddenly remembered that he was trying to convince her he had subconscious leanings toward male chauvinism. "I would never allow a woman to drive me anywhere. Women are terrible drivers. They're far too emotional," he added for good measure.

"Drivel, but if you want to think that, it's fine by me. I don't like to drive."

Kali glanced around as Hassan turned into the parking lot of a large shopping mall. There wasn't a ski slope in sight.

"Where are we?" she asked.

"There's a good ski shop in this mall, and I thought I'd get you some proper equipment." *Wrong phrasing,* Hassan thought, critiquing his performance. He hadn't sounded emphatic enough.

"You wouldn't know what to buy if I left it up to you," he tried again.

"True enough," Kali said calmly.

Hassan subsided into silence, not sure if he was making progress. She hadn't sounded annoyed with his dogmatic pronouncement, but he couldn't expect her to sud-

denly realize he was a chauvinist when he hadn't acted
that way before.

Hassan pulled the car into a parking space near the
entrance and walked around to open her door for her.

Kali gave in to her sudden impulse and placed a quick
kiss on his cheek. Her lips seemed to momentarily cling
to his warm skin.

"What does the well-dressed skier wear these days?"
Kali struggled to keep her sexual longing out of her
voice as she fell into step beside him.

"You don't need to worry about it. I'll tell you what
to buy."

She gave him an impish grin. "Then I won't worry.
'Lead on, MacDuff.'"

Once inside, Hassan checked the directory in the center of the mall for the name of the ski shop Mohammed
had provided.

Quickly finding it, he turned back to Kali to find her
staring into the distance, a frown on her face.

"What was that?" she asked.

Hassan looked around but didn't see anything except
a few shoppers. None of whom looked to be doing anything out of the ordinary.

"What's what?"

"That sound. It's…" She tilted her head to one side
and closed her eyes the better to listen. "It's coming
from that way." She pointed to her left.

Hassan looked. There were half a dozen good-size
trees in huge pots growing beneath an atrium. Scattered
around them were benches for the shoppers to rest on.

A small child of about three was huddled at the end
of one of them, crying. Hassan automatically started toward her.

His eyes swept over the other benches, wondering

who she belonged to. The ones nearest the little girl were empty, but farther away they were filled. Filled with people who were ignoring her.

"I've heard of people not wanting to get involved, but ignoring a crying kid is inexcusable," he snapped.

Strangely enough, Hassan's obvious anger helped to defuse Kali's. It didn't matter that a bunch of strangers refused to help the child. What mattered was that Hassan clearly shared her sense of outrage.

Stopping in front of the weeping child, Kali gave her a warm smile and said, "Hi, there."

The child looked up, wiped her runny nose on the sleeve of her pink jacket, studied Kali for a long moment and then turned to Hassan.

Hassan responded to the doubt he could see in the child's face by squatting down in front of her so their eyes were on the same level.

"What's wrong?" Kali sat down beside the child.

The little girl inched away slightly, hiccuped and then muttered, "I's lost."

"No, you're not," Hassan said cheerfully. "You're sitting on a bench in the atrium in the mall."

The little girl considered his words. Finally she gave him a tentative smile.

"I'll bet the grown-up you're with has gone and gotten themselves lost," Hassan continued.

"Must be," Kali added, "because I can't see them anywhere."

"My mommy," the little girl muttered. "I can't find her nowhere!" Her voice broke on a sob.

Kali resisted the impulse to put her arms around the little girl and comfort her. She had undoubtedly been warned never to let a stranger touch her, and to do so, even with the best of intentions, would undoubtedly scare the child even more.

"Why don't we take her to mall security?" Hassan suggested.

"She can't go with us because we're strangers," Kali whispered to Hassan. "Children have to be taught never to go anywhere with strangers."

"Seems to me we'd do better to try to teach the mother never to take her eyes off her daughter!"

Noticing the little girl's eyes widen at the exchange, Kali gave Hassan a warning glance before she turned back to the child.

"Where did you lose your mommy?" Kali asked.

"Mommy told me I could play in the toy store while she went to get Grandma's present. She said she'd come back and get me when she was done, but the toy fell off the shelf and the man got mad. I didn't mean to knock it off!" The child's voice rose with the vehemence of her denial. "It just fell."

"Of course you didn't," Hassan's deep voice flowed soothingly over the agitated child. "It was just one of those things. The clerk should have understood."

"Right," Kali seconded the sentiment. "So then what happened?"

"The mean man told me to go away, and I did. I tried to find my mommy, but I couldn't." The child's lower lip began to quiver again.

"Which store did your mommy go into?" Hassan asked.

"Down there." The child pointed vaguely toward the end of the mall.

"We'll have to—ah-ha! The cavalry!" Kali spotted a security guard, who had just come out of a store.

The little girl giggled. "You talk funny."

"He can talk even funnier." Kali stood up. "He'll show you while I go get that guard."

Hassan sat down in the seat Kali had vacated and began to recite the Hippocratic oath in Arabic. The child's eyes widened in amazement at the incomprehensible flow of words, and Kali hurried away.

She was back a few minutes later with the guard.

"Hi, there, kiddo." The man gave the child a comforting smile. "This lady tells me you need a little help."

The child eyed him a few minutes and then asked, "Is you really the cavalry?"

"Sure am. I'm John Wayne's right-hand man. Now if you'll just tell me your name, kiddo, I'll call the office on my phone here. They can make an announcement over the PA system."

"Madison Reilly," the little girl said, and the guard repeated it into his phone. A second later it was announced on the PA system.

"There," the man said in satisfaction. "That should bring your mommy running." The man turned to Kali. "You can safely leave her to me now."

"No!" Madison looked scared. "I don't want them to go yet. Not till my mommy comes."

"And unless I miss my guess, Mommy has just appeared on the horizon." Kali pointed to the woman carrying a large shopping bag and wearing a scowl, hurrying toward them.

"Where did you go to, Madison?" the woman demanded the second she reached them. "I told you to wait at the toy store. And I also told you never to talk to strange men!" The woman glared at Hassan.

"I would like to speak to you a moment, madam."

Hassan's voice was icy cold. "Over there." He nodded to a bench a few feet off.

"I don't think—"

"A masterly summation of your actions so far!" Kali snapped, furious at the woman's attitude toward Hassan.

"Now!" Hassan's voice held the authority of centuries of rulers who had held the power of life and death over their subjects.

The woman shot an angry look at the security guard, who simply stared back at her, before she reluctantly trailed after Hassan.

"Madam, I don't know if you are too stupid or too naive to know the dangers of leaving a small child alone in a store—"

"I told her to stay there," the woman said, defending herself.

"A harried store clerk is not a baby-sitter."

"I don't see what business it was of yours, anyway," the woman snapped. "Nobody asked you to interfere."

"I interfered, as you put it, because I am a pediatrician and it is my duty to see to the welfare of children. It is also my legal responsibility to report child abuse to the authorities."

"How dare you!" the woman sputtered angrily. "I have never, ever hit Madison."

"Abuse includes failure to provide a safe environment, and dumping a small child in a store and leaving her there certainly falls into that category."

"I didn't think—" The woman broke off when she remembered Kali's response to that bit of self-justification.

"Please do so in the future," Hassan said. "For Madison's sake, if not your own."

The woman sniffed and marched back to Madison. Grabbing the child's arm, she dragged her away.

The guard watched her go in disbelief. "What's with that woman? Surely she could have thanked you?"

"She's furious because she knows she was wrong," Kali said. "And it's when people know they're wrong that they're at their most obnoxious."

"She certainly was that," the guard agreed. "And don't worry about something like this happening again, folks. I'll talk to that clerk over in the toy store about calling Security when parents leave their kids there instead of making them leave. Good night."

"Thanks," Kali said to Hassan once the guard had left.

"For what?" Hassan asked.

Kali smiled at him. "Oh, just for being the kind of man who is willing to stop and help a kid. And for trying to talk some sense into her mother's head."

Hassan felt himself warm under the approving gleam in her eyes. "Unfortunately, I doubt that it did much good," he admitted honestly.

Kali slipped her arm through his and momentarily pressed it against her body, trying to comfort him.

"Don't be so pessimistic. Once she stops being embarrassed, she'll start to think, and common sense should make her very hesitant to leave Madison on her own again.

"Now then, let's go get my ski equipment."

Hassan headed toward the ski shop, mentally scrambling to make the transition from concerned pediatrician to overbearing male.

Kali dealt his plans a severe setback when she looked around the piles of equipment in the shop and said,

"You pick, Hassan. I haven't the vaguest idea what to buy."

Thwarted, Hassan quickly assembled a sizable pile of professional-quality equipment, much to the delight of the hovering salesman.

"And you'll need a jacket and pants, too," Hassan said.

Kali studied the rack of outfits the clerk obligingly pointed out to her, her eyes lingering on a forest-green one.

Hassan noticed her interest and hurried to further his plan.

"Not that one," he stated emphatically. "Get that red one." He pointed to a brilliant scarlet outfit hanging on the wall.

Kali eyed it consideringly for a long moment. "You're probably right. If I'm wearing something that bright, I'll be much easier to find and dig out of snow-banks."

Hassan chuckled in spite of his frustration at the ease with which she kept deflecting his chauvinistic pronouncements.

"Don't worry," the clerk told her as he began to total what they'd chosen. "We haven't lost a skier to an avalanche yet. What you got to watch out for are the trees."

"Trees?" Kali repeated blankly. "Why? They stay in one spot, don't they?"

The clerk nodded. "Unfortunately skiers don't. Sometimes they hit them. Why, just last year some guy from New York City hit a tree going over fifty miles an hour at that big resort up the road."

Kali gulped, not liking the image that came to mind.

"It won't be a problem." Hassan instinctively responded to the worry he could see shimmering in her eyes. "You can start out on a nice gentle slope without any trees at all."

Kali relaxed slightly at his words. He had sounded as if he knew what he was doing, and she was more than willing to be guided by his experience, since she didn't have any of her own to draw on.

"There we are." The clerk finished ringing in their purchases. "Will you be using a credit card?"

Yes, and it was going to be a while before she did so again, Kali thought, barely suppressing a shudder at the total.

She pulled out her credit card a second before Hassan found his.

"I'll pay for it," he said.

"After we're married you can pay," Kali said, and Hassan was momentarily distracted by the intoxicating images that flooded his mind at the thought of being married to her. It was long enough for the clerk to accept Kali's card.

He'd send her a check, Hassan thought, assuaging his guilt at having inadvertently stuck her with the bill for all this equipment. He wanted to break her engagement, not her bank account.

"How far is Faisal's place?" Kali asked, once they were back on the road.

"About half an hour north of here."

"Time enough for me to check with my answering service." She fished her portable phone out of her purse. "I told one of my teenaged patients this afternoon that she could call the service if she needed me, and I'd call her back as soon as I could."

Hassan listened to the sound of Kali's voice as she

talked into the phone. She was a very caring, nurturing woman.

She'd make a wonderful mother, Hassan thought. Patient and kind. She wouldn't be the type to sweat the small stuff. Her children would grow up knowing that their mother loved them and cared enough to set limits, but they'd also have the space they needed to develop as individuals.

The knowledge unexpectedly depressed him, and it took all his considerable willpower to banish his thoughts and concentrate instead on driving on the snowy roads.

Finally reaching Faisal's estate, he pulled into the parking area and climbed out of the car.

"You'd best put on your chador before we go in," he said. "Faisal will expect it."

There was no best about it, Kali thought, as she struggled to drape the unwieldy thing over her coat.

Once she was swathed from head to toe in badly wrinkled black silk, Hassan handed Kali her bag of ski equipment, got their cases out of the trunk and then headed toward the lodge, which was brilliantly illuminated by the lit ski area on the left.

"This is a private residence?" Kali studied the huge house in surprise. "It looks more like a high-class resort."

"I think it was before Faisal bought it."

Kali tried to imagine what it would be like to have enough money to be able to buy a ski resort and then run it simply as a winter vacation home, and failed.

What did this Faisal do for a living? Kali wondered. And what could he possibly have in common with the Rashid family? She knew Karim worked very hard as a research scientist, but what did Hassan do for a living?

Her thoughts came to a sudden halt as she remembered the man injured in the truck crash. Was Hassan some kind of a medical doctor? It would certainly explain how he'd known how to do an emergency tracheotomy.

"What's wrong?" Hassan peered over his shoulder at Kali, wondering at her arrested expression. Was she starting to have second thoughts about the weekend?

"Um, nothing," she muttered, knowing there was no way she could find out without also letting him know that she knew he wasn't Karim. Something she had to avoid at all costs, because once his deception was out in the open everything would be over between them.

Besides, it didn't really matter what Hassan did for a living. What mattered was the type of man he was—kind and compassionate and caring and smart and funny and sexy. Especially sexy.

"You look…odd," Hassan persisted.

Kali gave him what she hoped was a natural smile. "I was just wondering what Faisal does for a living."

"Collects royalties."

Kali frowned. "He's an author?"

Hassan chuckled.

"Not those kind of royalties. Oil royalties. As far as I know Faisal's never done anything useful in his life." That should serve as an object lesson to Kali on the horrors of having a Middle-Eastern husband, Hassan thought.

"But what—" Kali paused as the front door swung open before they could knock.

"Hassan, dear boy! Welcome. Welcome." A thin, elderly man greeted Hassan exuberantly. "I am so pleased that you are finally able to spend a weekend with me. I can't tell you how happy it makes me to be able to return your dear father's hospitality. And how is your father?''

Hassan set down their luggage, ignoring his desire to pull Kali forward and force Faisal to acknowledge her. This was exactly what he wanted, he reminded himself. For Faisal to be his usual, chauvinistic self.

"He's fine, sir. And I hope you are enjoying equal good health?''

"I can't complain,'' Faisal said.

I sure could, Kali thought. And I probably would if I had to put up with being totally ignored on a regular basis.

"John here will show you to your rooms,'' Faisal nodded toward the pudgy young man standing to one side of the doorway. "Then you can join me in the library, Hassan.''

"I want to get in some skiing tonight,'' Hassan hastily said, wanting to prolong the moment when he would be effectively separated from Kali. "Afterward I will.''

"Fine, fine.'' Faisal nodded happily. "The skiing is excellent for this early in the season. Till later then.''

Hassan took Kali's arm, and they followed John to the elevator at the end of the hallway.

"You know, Hassan, I'm beginning to have a great deal of fellow feeling for kids who throw temper tantrums simply to get attention. It's no fun feeling like you're invisible. If Faisal is a sample of the Middle-Eastern mentality, it's no wonder you chose to make your home in the West.''

Hassan felt a rising sense of frustration at her words, because that was exactly what he would have preferred to do, make his home in the West, and for exactly those reasons. And yet he couldn't. He was duty-bound to go home.

"You'll love skiing." Hassan took out his frustration in a dogmatic pronouncement.

Kali chuckled. "What odds are you giving?"

John stopped in front of a door three down from the elevator.

"The lady is in here, sir," John said. "Your room is on the floor above."

The devil take Faisal Sharif and his antiquated ideas! Kali thought.

Apparently reading her mind, John added, "Mr. Sharif's suite is in the other wing. He never comes over to the guests' side."

Kali smiled at the young man for that bit of information.

"I'll meet you downstairs in ten minutes, Kali," Hassan said.

"Do you mean Faisal will allow me to use the elevator all by myself?" Kali gave Hassan a look of wide-eyed shock.

John hastily turned a laugh into a choked cough, and Hassan took out his frustration by stomping off down the hall. He was short-tempered only because his life was so unsettled at the moment, he assured himself. Once he'd gotten Kali to break her engagement and he no longer saw her on a regular basis his emotions would revert to their normal even keel.

The thought brought him absolutely no comfort.

John gave Kali an irreverent thumbs-up sign and hurried after Hassan.

Feeling better, Kali pushed open her bedroom door and stepped inside. She barely noticed the room's blatant luxury as she upended her shopping bag of ski equipment on the oversize bed.

She wasted no time changing. She wanted to get back

to Hassan as soon as possible. She wanted to spend the evening with him, even if it meant freezing her fingers off and putting the rest of her limbs in danger of being broken. It was worth any risk to be with Hassan.

Nine

"Say, aren't you one of the Rashid—"

"Hassan Rashid." He hurriedly cut off the middle-aged man who had just emerged from the room to the left of the front door, afraid that he was about to blurt out the fact that he was one of a set of twins.

Hassan stole a quick glance toward the elevator looking for Kali. To his relief, the hallway was still empty.

"I thought I recognized you. I'm Milton Karnov from Trans-World Oil. I've done quite a bit of business with your father, and I hope to do even more in the future."

Karnov pumped Hassan's hand with a great deal of enthusiasm. An enthusiasm Hassan did not share.

When he'd decided to spend the weekend at Faisal's, he'd thought it would be enough to ask Faisal not to mention that he had a twin brother. He'd never even considered the fact that Faisal might have Westerners visiting him. Westerners who might recognize him and, even more worrying, who would see nothing wrong in talking to Kali.

"You're the one who's a doctor, aren't you?" Karnov asked.

"Yes," Hassan replied, trying to keep his eye on the elevator without being obvious about it. It was already a few minutes past the time when he was supposed to meet Kali here, and she was usually prompt.

"That's great! I have the most awful pain in my back, and it just won't go away. What do you think I should do about it?"

Hassan tensed as the elevator doors slid open to reveal Kali.

"It sounds like you need to see an orthopedic surgeon," Hassan hurriedly said.

"Probably, but I can't do that till I go back to New York City on Monday. Couldn't you look at it?"

"No," Hassan said, wishing Karnov were in New York City at the moment. "Never trust your back to anyone less than an expert."

Hassan turned as Kali reached them.

"Milton Karnov, Kali Whitman," Hassan said, seeing no way to avoid the introduction. If he ignored Karnov, Kali would be bound to wonder why, and the situation was volatile enough without her becoming curious about him.

Hassan gave Karnov a cold glare in the hope that the poor man would think that he was being typically possessive about his woman talking to a strange man. That way maybe Karnov wouldn't say anything beyond social pleasantries for fear of offending Hassan, and through him, his father.

"Miss Whitman," Karnov gave her a polite, but distinctly reserved smile, and Hassan felt his tension ease slightly. Karnov appeared to have caught the hint. But before Hassan could hustle Kali out the door, Faisal emerged from a room farther down the hall and, seeing Hassan, rushed toward him.

"Hassan, my boy, I see Milton has introduced himself to you."

"Oh, Hassan and I have met before," Karnov said. "His father and I—"

"You've traveled in the Middle East, Mr. Karnov?" Kali hurriedly interrupted, afraid that Karnov was about to blurt out who Hassan really was. Once he did that, Hassan's masquerade would be over and with it even her slight chance of getting Hassan to fall in love with her.

Faisal gave Kali an outraged glare for daring to interrupt a man, but she ignored him. On a list of things she had to worry about at present, offending Faisal ranked somewhere near the bottom.

"I work in the Middle East," Karnov said. "But I was just telling Hassan about my bad back. He suggested that I should see an orthopedic specialist."

Kali hurriedly latched on to the subject of medicine in the hopes of diverting the conversation into safer channels. "You really should see one before you leave the country again, because I would think medical specialties would be rather thin on the ground in the Middle East. Although, of course, I don't know that for a fact," she rushed on. "What is medicine like there?"

To her surprise, Faisal launched into a five-minute diatribe about how the lower classes in his country were demanding all kinds of expensive medical procedures that threatened to bankrupt the health care system.

"Every human being, no matter what their social class, has the right to the very best that modern medicine can provide," Hassan said, unable to keep quiet in the face of such comprehensive bigotry.

"Nonsense, my boy," Faisal blustered.

Kali carefully avoided looking around the opulent hallway of Faisal's vacation home. Clearly Faisal believed that conspicuous consumption was an acceptable use of money. At least it was acceptable when he was the one doing the consuming. But Kali knew that it wouldn't do the slightest bit of good to point out to him just how appallingly selfish he was being. A man like Faisal would never be moved by an appeal to his better nature. Always supposing he had one! The only way to ever get him to agree with what you wanted done was to firmly wed it to his own self-interest.

"Perhaps," Kali said. "But if you don't keep the lower classes healthy, they become a breeding ground for disease and once disease starts to spread it is no respecter of rank."

"Very true," Karnov seconded her words.

To Kali's surprise there was a twinkle of humor in Karnov's eyes, rather as if he knew what she was trying to do and appreciated her efforts even if he didn't think much of her chances.

"You Western women think you know everything," Faisal snapped, "but you know nothing, nothing at all, about conditions in the Middle East."

"If you'll excuse us, sir, we want to get in a little skiing before it gets too late." Hassan said.

Grabbing Kali's arm, Hassan hustled her out the front door, his mood precariously balanced between anger at Faisal's criminally selfish attitude and fear that his real identity might come out if the conversation continued much longer.

And the most frustrating thing about Faisal's attitude

was that it wasn't all that uncommon. Fully half the members of the so-called upper class in Saad Dev'a either secretly resented or actively resisted his father's determination that all the kingdom's citizens should share in the wealth that oil had brought.

And it wouldn't be very long before he'd be dealing with men who thought like Faisal on a daily basis. Hassan's jaw clenched at the disheartening prospect.

Kali studied his tense features as he grabbed two sets of skis from the well-stocked racks on the porch.

"You can't let people like Faisal get to you, Hassan," she said. "What he thinks doesn't really have any bearing on how you live your life."

If only it were true, Hassan thought grimly.

"Let's forget the blasted man," Kali said. "You were going to give me a skiing lesson."

Hassan made a determined effort to throw off his bad mood so that he could concentrate on Kali.

"We'll start on this slope." Hassan headed toward the gentle hill beside the house. "It looks about right for a beginner."

They were almost to the base of the hill when there was a sudden shriek as a skier toppled over and came sliding down the slope on his back.

Kali watched in sympathy as the man finally reached the bottom. A tall young man skied up to the fallen man and helped him to his feet. The skier responded to whatever his rescuer had said by emphatically shaking his head and tramping off toward the house.

"Do you think he's hurt?" she asked worriedly.

"No, if he'd hurt himself he couldn't have walked away."

"Why don't I find that fact comforting?" Kali muttered.

Hassan looked down into her worried features and squelched the impulse to tell her that there was nothing to be afraid of. That she'd do just fine. That he wouldn't let anything happen to her.

He had to keep focused on his goal, he reminded himself, and ignoring her fears about learning to ski would be bound to reinforce the bad impression of Middle-Eastern men she had to be getting from Faisal.

Searching his memory for his father's exact tone when he was at his most imperious, Hassan said, "You will learn to ski."

Her infectious chuckle almost made him forget what he was trying to do.

"I want you to learn to ski," he tried again.

"So do I. I certainly don't want to have to stay behind while you're out skiing.

"Besides," she added, "being able to do that must be the next best thing to flying." She pointed farther up the mountain.

Hassan followed the direction of her finger and felt a flash of raw terror when he saw a skier skimming over the snow.

"Don't even consider it!" he ordered. "That man's clearly an expert. If you were to try that trail, you'd probably break your neck."

Kali felt warmed by the very real concern she could hear in his voice. Hassan cared for her. He might not love her, but he cared for her and was concerned about her safety. It was a solid foundation for her to build on. If only she could somehow finagle enough time to do it.

"Hi, there. Do you want to take a lesson?" The young man who'd rescued the fallen skier approached them. "I'm Jim. Mr. Sharif hired me to give lessons to his guests."

"I'm going to teach her," Hassan said, not liking the way the man was eyeing Kali...as if she were a particularly delectable dessert. It wasn't that he was jealous, he assured himself. He was simply trying to give Kali the impression he was jealous, because that would add to what should be her growing doubts about marrying him.

"Thanks, Hassan." Kali gave him a grateful smile once Jim had left. "That guy moves like he was born on skis. If I'm going to be falling all over the slopes, I'd prefer to have a friend watching. At least if you laugh at me, I can retaliate."

Hassan looked down into her sparkling eyes and felt the excitement that was never far beneath the surface when he was around her skyrocket. She looked as if she knew a tantalizing secret that she was considering sharing with him.

"What kind of retaliation?" he asked.

"Just be careful you don't wound my tender little sensibilities and find out."

"Are your sensibilities tender?"

Kali tilted her head to one side as if considering it and finally said, "About as tender as the next person's. Now I think we'd better get on with this lesson, because my fingers are starting to go numb."

Hassan frowned. "They shouldn't be. Not in those gloves." He grabbed her right hand and, removing her glove, studied her fingers.

She had nice hands, he thought. Soft, with neatly rounded nails coated with a clear polish instead of the garishly painted talons that so many women boasted these days.

He put her hand against his cheek to check the temperature of her fingers, but the feel of her skin against his, effectively shattered his professional interest. All he could think about was how he'd felt when she'd run her fingers over his bare back as they'd made love.

Unconsciously he turned his head and pressed a kiss on her palm. He inhaled the very faint fragrance of roses.

"Um, I thought you were going to give me a skiing lesson," Kali muttered.

Skiing wasn't what he wanted to teach her, Hassan thought. In fact, skiing was...a vehicle to impose his chauvinism on her, he reminded himself, a sense of desperation rising. What was the matter with him? Why couldn't he keep focused on his goal? Why did he seem to forget what he had to do every time Kali so much as glanced his way.

He didn't know, and this clearly wasn't the time to worry about it, he told himself.

"They don't feel all that cold to me." He struggled to sound dismissive.

"You're probably one of those aggravating individuals who turn the heat down to sixty-two in the winter, too," she grumbled. "Well, since I can't get any sympathy, let's get on with it."

"Right." Hassan glanced around the deserted slope. Not looking at her helped his concentration.

Dropping their skis on the snow, he helped her put hers on and then fastened his own.

"Aren't I supposed to have poles?" Kali asked. "They always do on television."

"Poles give the beginner a false sense of security," Hassan quoted his own childhood instructor.

"I'll take any kind of feeling of security, false or not," she said, but he ignored her.

"Let's go up to the top of the beginners' slope." He slid forward, stopping when he heard a squeak behind him.

He turned to find Kali madly flailing her arms around in an attempt to keep her balance. One of her skis had crossed over the other at the tip.

Hassan fought to control his urge to laugh at her surprised expression. Male chauvinists weren't supposed to have a sense of humor.

"You're supposed to keep the edges of your skis parallel," he said.

"Stuff the theory! Give me some practical advice on how to do it."

"Carefully," he said. "It's a skill that comes with practice."

"Always provided I live long enough to get it."

"Straighten them out." Hassan waited until she had accomplished it. "Now push your skis forward, one at a time."

Kali tried again, this time managing to move a few feet forward.

"I did it!" She beamed at him.

She started forward again, carried along on a wave of enthusiasm. Unfortunately it didn't carry her far. She crossed her skis again, overbalanced and fell.

Hassan reached down and pulled her to her feet.

Kali rubbed the snow out of her face and righted her bright red ski cap which had fallen over her left ear. This time she moved very cautiously, slowly inching forward.

Hassan watched, a bit surprised at her persistence. She might not have been that eager to learn, but having committed herself, she was giving it her best.

His eyes narrowed thoughtfully as he wondered what else she might be willing to try. A warmth trickled through his loins as several intriguing possibilities occurred to him.

He watched as Kali continued to inch her way toward the crest of the gentle slope. By the time she reached the top she was gasping for breath.

This is ridiculous, she told herself. She shouldn't be this out of breath from a little bit of simple exercise. She was going to see about enrolling in some kind of fitness program on Monday so she'd be able to keep up with Hassan.

She slowly ran her tongue over her lower lip as she eyed the width of his broad shoulders beneath the down-filled blue ski jacket he was wearing. They looked enormous. A shiver raced through her that had nothing to do with the frigid night air.

"Turn around." Hassan's sudden order jerked her out of her erotic thoughts and, startled, she spun around.

Her awkward movement overbalanced her again, and to her shock Kali felt her skis began to move, taking her with them.

"Keep your skis parallel!" She heard Hassan shout as she began to pick up speed.

"And how am I supposed to do that, when I can't even get my own body to do what I want it to?" she muttered to herself.

"Get away!" Kali shrieked when the ski instructor suddenly swooped down beside her.

Her instinctive attempt to wave him off doomed her efforts to stay upright, and she pitched over, rolling to the bottom in a tangle of arms, legs and skis.

"Are you all right?" Jim reached her first.

"Don't move!" Hassan's harsh voice came a second later. He sounded furious.

"I don't know what you've got to be annoyed at," she told Hassan. "I'm the one who fell." She lifted an arm to try to lever herself up.

"I told you not to move!" Hassan said, running his hands over her limbs. "Does anything hurt?"

Hurt? Kali closed her eyes and searched inwardly. The only thing she could feel was the delicious sensation of his hard fingers pushing against her skin. It felt fantastic. Hurt didn't come into it at all.

"Kali!"

"Sorry." Reluctantly she opened her eyes. "I'm fine."

"You're sure," Jim persisted. "Mr. Sharif would be very upset if I let one of his guests break something."

"Don't worry, I'm fine." Kali took the hand Hassan offered her and struggled to her feet, trying to keep from tripping over the skis again. "Haven't you heard? We women are a pretty sturdy lot."

"To say nothing of impetuous." Hassan repositioned her skis so that they were both pointing in the same direction. "Whatever made you take off like that?"

Kali giggled. "Surely you don't think that plunge downhill was voluntary, do you? I think my skis are possessed. Kind of like a Stephen King novel."

After one quick glance at her laughing features, Hassan hastily averted his gaze. He absolutely couldn't afford to share her amusement. Duty and humor were not compatible. At least, not in his life they weren't.

"I think you should call it a night, miss," Jim said. "You can tackle the slope again in the morning when you're fresh."

"No." Hassan said. "She can't give up now."

"But—" Jim began.

"He's right." Kali smiled at the worried-looking young man. "I think this is a case of that old cliché about getting right back up when you fall off a horse. I need to show myself that I can do it."

Jim shrugged. "If that's what you want, but if you should need me, just sing out." He gave Hassan a disapproving scowl and moved away.

Hassan studied the determined jut of Kali's fragile-looking chin, realizing that Kali wasn't the least bit fragile. She had a core of tempered steel. She wasn't about to let herself be bested by a ski slope. A feeling of pride at her spunk washed through him, and his voice softened.

"This time you go first, and I'll follow."

Kali eyed him uncertainly. "But what happens if I slide back into you?"

"You'll come to a sudden stop."

Kali took a deep breath. She could do this. Skiing was nothing more than the mastering of a few of the basic laws of physics, and she'd always been very good at physics.

With a feeling of determination she turned and began a tortuously slow crawl up the slope. This was as good a way as any to pass the time until night.

Just because Faisal had put them in separate rooms didn't mean they had to stay in separate rooms. Not if she had anything to say about it.

Kali shot a quick glance over her shoulder at Hassan's beloved features and almost fell.

"Careful." He steadied her with a hand on her back. "Keep your concentration."

I am, she thought. *It's just that I'm concentrating on your lovemaking and not on my skiing.*

"We'll quit after this run," Hassan said even though he knew he should insist that she continue skiing. But it wasn't going to help his cause any if Kali were to have an accident and hurt herself, he thought, rationalizing his desire to protect her.

"Okay." Kali gamely tried to increase her snail-like pace.

She finally got to the top of the slope, and this time she managed to slide almost to the bottom before her skis crossed and she fell.

"For the life of me I can't see how you can manage those things," she complained as Hassan hauled her to her feet again.

"I told you, experience. It'll come in time." Kneeling, he helped her out of her skis.

"Maybe," she said doubtfully, "but I sure could use some help in the meantime. They ought to make skis that fasten together to keep them from crossing."

"But then you wouldn't have any freedom of movement."

"Good. From where I'm standing, or, more accurately, falling, my problems are caused by too much freedom of movement."

Unable to resist the impulse, Hassan dropped a quick kiss on her pink lips. They tasted invigorating, like the outdoors itself.

"Let's hurry. My fingers are frozen. I want to get them warm." She fell into step beside Hassan as he shouldered their skis and headed back to the lodge.

Her fingers wouldn't be the only thing that would be warm after an evening spent in Faisal's home, Hassan thought. Her temper would quickly reach the boiling point, too. Although…

The memory of her calm reaction to Faisal's earlier rudeness flickered through his mind, suddenly making him uncertain.

"I'll ask Faisal where the women are," Hassan told her once they were back inside.

"If they've got any sense they're hiding from the little twirp," she muttered under her breath.

"There you are, Hassan!"

As if on cue, Faisal emerged from the room to the right of the entrance hall. "I had a couple of new releases flown in from Hollywood this morning. We're about to watch one."

Faisal gave Kali a sideways glance as if he couldn't bear to look directly at her and added, "The subject content is not suitable for women."

Kali gave him a gentle smile. "Somehow, that doesn't surprise me."

Hassan choked back a laugh at Faisal's confused expression. Clearly Faisal wasn't sure whether Kali was being conciliatory or whether she was mocking him.

"Go ahead and start without me," Hassan said. "I'll take Kali to her room and be down later."

As much later as I can get away with, Hassan thought. Spending the entire evening with Faisal and his contemporaries was more than he could face at the moment. And yet it was precisely with men like Faisal that he would be spending the rest of his life. The knowledge made his feet drag as he escorted Kali to the elevator.

When they reached her room, Hassan sifted through all the things he wanted to say but couldn't, and finally muttered an anemic sounding, "If you want anything, you can call me on the house phone."

And who was he supposed to call to make his world right? Hassan wondered grimly as he shoved his bedroom door open.

He dropped into an armchair and closed his eyes, trying to distance himself from the frustrations that swirled through him. An image of Kali's face immediately floated in front of him. She was such a unique woman; it was no wonder he was in love with her.

His totally unexpected self-discovery slammed through his mind with numbing force, leaving him confused and uncertain.

Could he really be in love with her? He tried to think.

He certainly liked her and shared her sense of humor. He admired her intelligence and the work she was doing with her young patients. He lusted after her fantastic body.

He jumped to his feet and began to pace the room, too agitated to sit still. But it was more than just sex that he craved, he realized. He wanted to cherish her and protect her from anything that would harm her. He wanted to make plans for the future with her. To have children with her. To come home to her every night. He wanted to grow old with her. And when he died, he wanted her beloved face to be the image he carried into paradise.

Hassan drew a jagged breath, squarely facing the fact that if he couldn't share his life with Kali, he didn't think his life would be worth living. Desperately he tried to figure out what he should do.

He couldn't. He couldn't get beyond the panicky thought that without Kali he'd never be anything more than a robot, mindlessly going through the motions of living.

But he'd promised his father that he would return to the kingdom.

Hassan made a monumental effort to think. To try to remember exactly when and why he'd made that promise.

It had been almost twenty years ago.

His father had just returned from England where he'd

seen his ex-wife, and it had been obvious to the teenage Hassan that he was feeling down. Hassan had wanted to comfort him. To cheer him up. To make him forget his wife's defection.

Now for the first time, Hassan took a long, hard look at his parents' marriage from the viewpoint of a dispassionate adult and not through the eyes of a hurt child who'd been emotionally crushed by his mother's flat refusal to accompany them back to the kingdom after his uncle's untimely death.

His father had been faced with the unenviable choice between what he saw as his duty to his country and his fealty to his wife, who refused to live permanently in a place she hated. And his father had chosen duty over his love for his wife. Something Hassan found inexplicable. Kali and his love for her were the most important things in his life. Everything else paled to insignificance.

Hassan frowned. He didn't know if his father had been swayed by the very real power he'd gained—both political and economic. Or even if his father had believed that his wife would capitulate in the end, but the fact remained that his father had chosen the kingdom over his wife. And just as his father had made his choice, he was now faced with the same choice. But it wasn't a choice his father had asked him to make, Hassan realized. He hadn't asked any of his sons to make that sacrifice.

What would be the consequences if he didn't return? Hassan wondered. It wouldn't impact negatively on the smooth running of the kingdom because he wouldn't be doing anything that couldn't be done by someone else…that wasn't already being done by someone else. He remembered his father had hired Fayed's young relative to temporarily run the country's hospitals. His father could offer the job of administrator to the man on a permanent basis. From the sound of things, he'd be glad to accept.

His father had always intended that his eldest son, Ali, inherit the throne after him. So his not returning would not upset the succession.

And he could offer to spend one weekend a month in the kingdom overseeing the job the man was doing. That way if there were ever any problems, he would be aware of them early enough to correct them before there were repercussions.

A flicker of hope sparked to life deep within him. It might work. It would be a way for him to help shoulder some of the burden of the kingdom and yet still marry Kali.

Hastily he strode toward the door, coming to a sudden stop as reality dampened his first burst of hope.

Just because he wanted to marry Kali didn't mean that she wanted to marry him. She'd been going to marry Karim, and Karim was a very outgoing, extroverted type of man. If Karim's personality appealed to her, would his own, far more reserved one?

The only way to find out would be to ask. His stomach churned at the thought of telling Kali the truth. Once he did that there would be no going back. If she didn't want to marry him, he'd never see her again.

But as much as he wanted to postpone his confession so that he could have at least a few more days in her company, he knew the risk was too great. If she were to find out his real identity from either Karnov or Faisal, she might be so angry she wouldn't listen to anything he had to say.

How should he go about telling her? He tried out several approaches as he slowly made his way back down the stairs to her room.

Hi, Kali. I just came back to mention the fact that I'm not really Karim. I'm his twin brother, but let's get married anyway. He winced at how flip he sounded. Somehow he needed to convince her of his sincerity. Maybe something like, *I'm not really Karim, but I love you and want to marry you? Please?*

Filled with uncertainty, he chewed his lower lip.

The problem was that Kali was liable to be so mad when he confessed his impersonation that she wouldn't listen to anything else he had to say.

Hassan grimaced. There was something to be said for the good old days. Then he could have just kidnapped her and held her captive in the desert somewhere until she agreed to marry him.

Pausing in front of her door, he sent up a silent prayer for success and then knocked.

Kali opened it immediately, and Hassan eagerly searched her beloved face, looking for some sign that she shared his love. He couldn't find any. She looked her normal, enticing self.

"I wanted to talk to you." He forced the words out past a throat almost closed with tension.

Kali felt an icy chill spread through her at his rigid expression.

Bracing herself, she gestured into the room. "Come in."

Had he finally decided to tell her who he really was? Kali swallowed against her stomach's sudden panicked lurch.

"I…" Hassan shoved his hand through his hair, clearly at a loss as to where to start, and Kali felt her spirits plummet still farther.

Her first guess had been right, she realized in despair. He was going to tell her the truth and ruin everything. Somehow she had to stop him.

Her gaze swung frantically around the room, looking for an inspiration. It came when her eyes landed on the bed. Maybe she could distract him by making love to him. Maybe that would get his mind off what he'd come for long enough for her to figure out what to do.

"I…" Hassan choked on the single word.

"You poor baby, you need to unwind," Kali murmured, hoping she didn't sound as nervous as she felt.

Hassan gulped. Her voice was an intoxicating mixture of sympathy and sexuality that turned his insides to a quivering mass of longing. It was becoming harder and harder to remember what he'd come here to do.

"What you need is the benefit of my one semester of massage therapy," she said.

"Massage therapy?" His words sounded strangled in his own ears.

"Uh-huh." Kali gently pushed him into the chair he was standing in front of and then walked around to the back of it.

He tipped his head back to follow her movement and was treated to the sight of her breasts outlined in the fuzzy blue sweater she was wearing. He hastily lowered his gaze, desperately trying to focus on what he had to say.

He couldn't make love to her until after he'd told her who he really was. He knew it. It wouldn't be right otherwise.

His thoughts suffered a dislocating blow when Kali placed her hands on his shoulders.

"You're tense as a board. You need to relax." Kali dug her fingertips into the tight muscles of his shoulders.

Hassan gulped, feeling his body beginning to react. If Kali thought touching him was going to make him relax, she'd probably flunked her massage course!

Her fingers inched upward, lightly working their way over his neck until her hands cupped his chin. She began to slowly rub erotic circles on the sensitive skin behind his ears with her thumbs. He gasped at the volatile sensations that flooded him.

"Any better?" she asked.

Tell her, his conscience screamed at him, but her fingers began to move, and his thoughts fragmented into a million tiny, irretrievable pieces.

"I have this fantasy about being a masseuse," she murmured. "Did you ever fantasize about being one?"

"No." The sound of his voice echoed in his ears as if it were coming from a great distance. "But I do have this fantasy about having my own houri. You'd be perfect."

"I'm not quite sure exactly what a houri is," she murmured as her fingers continued to work their insidious magic on his body.

"A houri is a beautiful, seductive woman who lives only to please her master."

Kali's chuckle dropped into his whirling thoughts, raising his body temperature.

"Thank you. I've always wanted to be thought of as a beautiful, seductive woman."

Kali gently tugged his chin up, tilting his head back so she could look into his eyes. "Do you really think I could fulfill all your fantasies?"

She could fulfil fantasies he hadn't even had yet, Hassan thought. A lifetime wouldn't be long enough. But would she want to once he told her the truth? The thought put a brake on his growing ardor.

"If you have to think about it that hard, then I probably couldn't."

Hassan reacted instinctively to the uncertainty he
could hear in her voice. Turning, he caught her around
the waist and pulled her into his lap. He didn't want to
raise doubts about her own sensuality. First, he'd reas-
sure her and then he'd tell her the truth.

Staring down into her face, he said, "I don't have the
slightest doubt about your ability to fulfill all my fantasies."

Hassan shifted slightly as the warm, soft weight of her
in his lap was having the inevitable results. He could
feel her shoulder pressing against his chest, pushing at
his self-control. His arms tightened slightly, and she
snuggled trustingly against him, raising a myriad of feelings, from guilt at his deception to plain old lust.

"What's the matter?" Kali asked. "Am I too heavy?"

"Heavy? Where?" He indulged his compulsion to
touch her by running his hand along her shoulder and
then down over her small breast.

She trembled, and he felt an answering response deep
inside himself.

The rapid beating of her heart slammed into his palm,
and he pressed harder. He could feel her nipple hardening, and he had an overwhelming desire to see her
breast. To feast his eyes on the pale perfection of her
velvety skin. To kiss the rosy tip and then to take it in
his mouth and suckle it.

His breathing developed a hitch when she twisted
sideways.

Slipping her hand beneath his sweater, she pushed upward over his chest.

Kali tugged his head down and began to nuzzle the
skin behind his ear. Her lips felt fantastic, warm and firm

and infinitely alluring. When she caught his earlobe in her teeth and licked the tip, he jerked spasmodically.

He tried to think. Was she reassured enough for him to tell her the truth now?

His concentration suffered a further setback when she traced her lips along his jawline.

"You're not relaxing." Her seductive voice made a mockery of the words.

Relax? Hassan thought. A misogynist couldn't relax this close to such a beautiful, sexy woman.

"But you're in luck," Kali continued, "because I am going to give you chapter two in my massage therapy class."

To his disappointment she suddenly scooted off his lap leaving him feeling bereft.

"Now the first thing we need to do is to loosen your clothes."

Kali knelt and began to untie his shoes.

Hassan looked down, fascinated by the way the lamplight struck reddish sparks off her gleaming hair. It looked as if glittering fairy dust had been sprinkled over her head.

Unable to resist the impulse, he reached out and ran his hand over her hair, the silky texture caressing his fingers.

"You are the most fascinating assortment of textures," he muttered his thoughts aloud.

"Thank you, kind sir." Kali tilted her head back and looked up at him, her eyes lingering on the sharply etched planes of his face. That he was reacting to her was obvious, but just how much she'd distracted him from what he'd come to say wasn't so clear. Nor was there any way for her to find out. About all she could do at this point was to continue with her seduction efforts. If she were successful, she'd at least have the memory of this night to cherish.

She fumbled at his shoelaces with fingers that seemed to be all thumbs, finally managing to get them undone. Impatiently yanking his shoes off, she tossed them aside. Peeling off his black socks, she flung them after the shoes.

"Proper circulation of air over the body is very important to the success of massage therapy," Kali hurriedly said when he opened his mouth. "If your skin is stifled, then it doesn't work."

"I didn't know that."

Probably because I just this minute made it up, Kali thought. But whoever had said that all was fair in love and war was right. Results were what was important, and the result she hoped for was to gain Hassan's love. No matter how improbable that outcome seemed at the moment.

"Stand up," Kali ordered, and Hassan obediently did.

She rocked back on her heels and stared up the length of him, allowing herself the momentary pleasure of simply looking at his magnificent body. Reaching up, she unbuckled his belt and pulled it free. It joined his shoes on the floor.

Quickly, not giving him time to retreat, she unbuttoned his pants and pulled down the zipper.

His only reaction was the sudden hiss of his indrawn breath. So far so good, she encouraged herself.

She gripped the edge of his sweater and pulled it up over his head. Studying the cream-colored polo shirt he was wearing beneath it for a second, she decided it had to go, too. She wanted to feel his chest against hers, and she couldn't do that if he was wearing a shirt.

She yanked the polo shirt over his head, managing to dishevel his hair in the process.

"Sorry," she muttered as she smoothed his hair back into place with her fingers. His hair felt crisp, and she swallowed uneasily, feeling her breasts begin to tingle as she remembered how his hair had felt against her bare skin.

Not yet. She throttled the urge. At the moment she didn't want to do anything that in a pinch she couldn't claim to be part of massage.

"Lie on the bed, facedown," she ordered Hassan as she kicked off her shoes.

Hassan obeyed with a promptness that encouraged her.

"In the middle of the bed," she said, and when he'd scooted over, she knelt on the bed beside him.

Taking a deep breath, Kali placed the palms of her hands on his shoulders and began to slowly knead his flesh. His skin was warm and supple beneath her moving fingers. Sensuous. Her eyelids felt heavy, and it was a distinct effort for her to keep them open. The air in the room felt thick. Almost visible. Kali took a deep breath, laboring to drag it into her lungs.

Slowly savoring the contact, she worked her way down his spine till she reached his waist and found her progress hampered by the pants he still wore.

Kali raised her head and studied him, her gaze lingering lovingly on his face. His eyes were closed but his features were taut as if he were under great pressure.

"You can't work through cloth," Hassan said. Raising his hips, he worked his pants and shorts down his legs and off his body. He tossed them over the end of the bed, but Kali didn't notice. Her attention focused on his now naked body.

He had the most fantastic physique, she thought, staring down at his lean hips. They were flat and muscular and totally masculine. She placed her hands flat on his buttocks and pushed her fingers into his flesh. She wanted—

Kali let out a startled squeak when Hassan suddenly rolled over and stared up at her. His eyes seemed to be burning with a sensuality that appealed to her far more than any actual fire ever could. She ran the tip of her tongue over her bottom lip, watching as his eyes followed her movement with a heart-stopping intensity.

Unable to sustain his burning gaze, her eyes dropped and she found herself staring at his swollen manhood.

"You aren't the least bit relaxed," she blurted her thoughts out loud, and then winced at the inanity of the statement.

"That's because you aren't a very relaxing person," he muttered. "In fact, you're damned unsettling."

"You haven't seen anything yet," Kali vowed.

Slipping off the side of the bed, she grasped the bottom of her soft blue sweater and slowly pulled it up.

The odd ringing in his ears reminded Hassan of the necessity of breathing, and he gulped in air, unable to take his eyes off the wispy lace of her bra which so inadequately covered her breasts. Longingly he studied the taut pink nipples that pushed against the creamy lace. He wanted to rip her bra off and free her breasts. But not for long. He wanted to capture them first with his hands and then with his mouth.

A muscle began to twitch beneath his left eye in time with his ragged breathing. Why he had come in the first place and the need to tell her the truth became just so many meaningless words as he stared at her fantastic body.

"Hurry up," he muttered as she reached for the button on the waistband of her slacks.

"But, Hassan," Kali gave him a slow, provocative smile that set his heart to slamming against his rib cage. "I'm trying to relax you, and you don't seem to be relaxed."

With an exaggerated slowness that put Hassan forcibly in mind of torture, Kali unzipped her gray slacks and allowed them to fall to the floor with a soft whooshing sound.

His eyes widened as he stared at the tiny lacy panties she was wearing.

"You match," he muttered and then winced at how gauche he sounded.

"Yes, but," Kali reached behind her and unfastened her bra, letting it drop, "now I don't match."

Hassan closed his eyes and tried to ignore the feeling that he was about to burst. He wasn't sure how much more of this he could take.

"And now, I match again."

Dimly, as if from a great distance he heard the sound of her voice, and he opened his eyes to find her standing naked before him.

He stared at her as desire fountained within him, swamping his senses.

Kali leaned toward him, and he reached for her, grabbing her slender body and pulling her down. She landed on top of him with the force of a bomb going off. Reaction poured through him, obliterating everything but the basic need to make her a part of him.

He grasped the back of her head and roughly captured her mouth. It wasn't enough so he shoved his tongue between her lips and began a sensual duel with hers.

Kali squirmed beneath him, her soft abdomen pressed

against his manhood. Hassan began to tremble uncontrollably. He had to have her. Now.

Rolling over, he clumsily positioned himself above her and pushed himself deep within her. The delicious sensation of her satiny skin closing around him made him shake uncontrollably.

"Hassan, you…I…" Kali's words echoed meaninglessly in his ears as she dug her heels in the bed and arched her body against him, taking him even deeper.

Her action shattered his few remaining tendrils of self-control. Reaction exploded in him sending him into a world where there was nothing but feeling. Oceans of feeling. Deeper and deeper he drove, driven by both his own sense of urgency and the sound of Kali's husky voice encouraging him.

Finally Kali gave a keening sound and went rigid beneath him an instant before his own pleasure overtook him.

When he could move again, he pulled her into his arms, kissed her and struggled to get the words out.

"I…"

"Go to sleep," Kali tried to stop him. She just wanted to savor the glow of their lovemaking. Especially if this was the last time they were to share it. Her arms instinctively tightened around him trying to hold him closer.

"Kali, I—I'm not Karim. I'm me, Hassan." The words seemed to explode from him.

Kali felt every muscle in her body tense as she tried to absorb the blow of what would come next. She could handle it, she tried to tell herself. But she knew it was a lie. The loss of Hassan would haunt her to the day she died. She didn't see how she was going to get through the rest of her life without him.

She should move out of his arms, she thought. It

would be easier to if she weren't so close to him. But her rigid muscles wouldn't obey her.

"Kali?" She heard the uncertain sound of Hassan's voice echoing in her ears, and she madly scrambled for something to say. For anything, even a trite saying that would hide just how badly his words were affecting her. She loved him too much to want him to feel even a fraction of the pain and grief she would feel.

Her mind was a total blank. She couldn't think of a single thing.

"Kali, I—I might not be Karim, but I love you."

Kali blinked, trying to understand what he was saying. That he loved her? Could it be true?

"How can you love me?" she forced herself to ask, trying to figure out which would be better, to lose him forever or to have him stay in her life because he felt sorry for her. Both seemed equally untenable situations.

"How could I not love you?" His voice was tight with strain. "You're everything I ever wanted in a wife."

"Wife?" Kali repeated through the roaring in her ears. He was asking her to marry him?

"Kali, we can make it work," he said, rushing on, trying to forestall a refusal. "I can work in New York, and you won't have to ever visit the Middle East unless you want to."

Kali briefly closed her eyes against the waves of faintness which swept through her. She felt as if she'd just been given a last-second reprieve from a death sentence. She didn't understand why or how he'd fallen in love with her, any more than she understood how or why she'd fallen in love with him. She simply accepted it as a priceless gift from a benevolent fate.

"I love you, Hassan Rashid, and all the rest of it is

just logistics,'' she said. ''Nothing else really matters as long as we're together.''

She gasped as his arms suddenly closed around her with crushing force. They loosened almost immediately, and he peered down into her face, his eyes gleaming with an emotion that sent a wave of anticipation through her.

''Tell me, my darling heart, what kind of logistics are involved in us having a few kids?''

Kali deliberately fluttered her eyelashes at him in a parody of a thirties vamp. Happiness was pouring through her in such waves that she didn't think she could contain it. She felt as if it would burst out of her body and sweep them both away. She wouldn't have believed that anyone could be this happy. To have both Hassan and the promise of his children.

''Come a little closer and I'll explain it to you,'' she whispered throatedly.

''How close?'' He nuzzled the satiny skin of her breast, and she shivered violently as longing tore through her. ''As close as this?''

''It'll do for a start,'' she murmured as she met his lips.

Epilogue

"**D**ad? Dad!"

Hassan glanced down at his young son's worried features and ruthlessly interrupted Kali's great-aunt's monologue on the appalling amount of makeup modern women insisted on wearing.

"Excuse me, Aunt Jane, but Jaimie needs to speak to me."

Aunt Jane nodded regally at Hassan, gave Jaimie a doting smile and hurried away to find another relative to lecture.

"What's wrong, Jaimie?" Hassan leaned toward the five-year-old. "Is all the company getting to be too much for you?"

Jaimie glanced around the huge double living room which was packed with relatives.

"No. Not 'actly." He inched closer to his father as one of his grandfather Rashid's sisters waved at him.

"'Cept for great-aunt Miriam. She keeps telling me what a cute little boy I am. And I'm not little. Not cute neither!'' he added emphatically. "It's about Mom. Sorta."

"Your mother?" Hassan's eyes automatically swung to the bow window where Kali was sitting on a chaise longue holding their new daughter while the family admired her.

His eyes met hers, and for a moment Hassan forgot everything in the wave of love that poured through him. He would never have believed that he could grow to love her more than he had on their wedding day, but he had. Eight years of marriage had broadened and deepened his love for Kali until it was the foundation of his whole world.

"Dad?" Jaimie reclaimed his attention, and Hassan turned back to him.

He studied his son's worried features wondering what was troubling him. Jaimie was normally such a happy child. Could he be worried about his place in the family now that he had a little sister?

"Jaimie, you know how much your mom and I love you, don't you?"

Jaimie gave him an impatient look. "I know that! But what about poor Eleanor?"

Poor Eleanor? Hassan weighed his son's description of his sister. "What about Eleanor?"

"Do you love her, too?"

"Of course I do. She's my daughter."

"But how can you, Dad?" Jaimie asked earnestly. "I mean, she's ugly. She's got no hair and no teeth. She's red, and she can't do anything but scream and make disgusting noises."

"She only looks like that because she's just five days

old,'' Hassan reassured him. ''She'll improve. Before you know it, she'll be beautiful.''

Jaimie glanced doubtfully over at his sister who was snuffling inelegantly into her mother's shoulder. ''As beautiful as Mom?''

Hassan looked at Kali's beloved features and felt his heart contract with love.

''Eleanor will be beautiful,'' he said softly. ''But no one could ever be as beautiful as your mother.''

''Okay.'' Jaimie looked relieved. ''If you say so.''

Oh, I do, Hassan thought, his eyes never leaving Kali's face. *I most certainly do.*

*   *   *   *   *

Silhouette Stars

Born this Month

Sean Connery, Elvis Costello, Patrick Swayze, Coco Chanel, Bill Clinton, Robert de Niro, Madonna, Danielle Steel, Magic Johnson, Princess Anne

Star of the Month

Leo

The year ahead is full of opportunity. You will need to make changes in your personal life in order to reap the benefits of all that is on offer. Career moves later in the year should bring financial benefits. Travel is also well aspected especially if taken in the autumn when it could well be linked to new relationships.

SILH/HR/0008a

Virgo

Events of last month should have made you wiser about exactly who you can trust. Having learnt this you should feel ready to move on in a positive and forgiving mood.

Libra

With renewed optimism you enter a new phase in which many of the problems that you have encountered lately vanish. A romantic relationship brings an added glow to your life.

 Scorpio

Your love life may have led you to neglect other areas of your life, although now you will be able to get the balance right. There could be exciting job opportunities coming your way.

Sagittarius

You have sailed into calmer waters after the upheaval of last month. You should feel pleased with the way you have handled yourself. You should start to move onwards and upwards, putting yourself in a stronger and more positive position.

 Capricorn

Changes in several areas of your life will cause a degree of tension. Take any offers of help and by the end of the month you should feel pleased with all you have managed to achieve.

Aquarius

Recently you have dealt with a great deal of upheaval. By mid month you should be reaping some of the benefits. A reunion with someone from your past may lead to a celebration.

Pisces

An excellent, positive month in which many of your plans will start to come to fruition. Friends and loved ones should be supportive and you may see a certain relationship in a very favourable light.

Aries

You should feel confident about the future and now that you have made the decision to move on you will be surprised how supportive those close to you are. Travel plans are well aspected, especially those connected with business.

 Taurus

There could be a few tricky moments as certain people seem determined to misinterpret what you are really saying. Take a break and allow the dust to settle and by the end of the month life will be back on track.

Gemini

Don't push yourself too hard as your batteries need recharging. This is an excellent time to take a break, catch up on family, or just relax at home pampering yourself. A lucky win late in the month gets you in the mood for celebrating.

 Cancer

After the upheaval of last month life quietens down and you can use the calm to assess what you do next. Your finances receive a boost and you may be able to buy something special.

**Look out for more
Silhouette Stars next month**

▼SILHOUETTE
DESIRE®

AVAILABLE FROM 18TH AUGUST 2000

TALL, DARK & TEXAN Annette Broadrick

Man of the Month

Successful bachelor Dan Crenshaw always steers clear of love and any talk of forever. But then he meets the girl-next-door from his past, Shannon Doyle. Can Shannon tempt Dan to once again believe in love?

CINDERELLA'S TYCOON Caroline Cross

The Millionaire's Club

When a mix-up at the sperm bank unexpectedly made Sterling Churchill a father-to-be, he gallantly stepped forward to marry shy Susan Wilkins. It was a marriage in name only—until he gave his bride a soul-spinning kiss…

HARD LOVING MAN Peggy Moreland

McCloud Brides

Meeting a family she never knew she had, spirited Lacey Cline is grateful to have sexy Travis Cordell's strong shoulder to lean on. Travis would do anything to protect this lady's heart, even if it meant risking his own…

SAIL AWAY Kathleen Korbel

When Lilly Kokoa encountered a rugged stranger with no memory, they were in real danger. But once the threat was over, would her lover be able to look past Lilly's plain-Jane appearance and see the beauty within?

STAR-CROSSED LOVERS Zena Valentine

They'd been childhood sweethearts…until tragedy ripped their relationship apart. Now Kale Noble and Jessi Caldwell are face-to-face again, their passion still simmering—and Jessi's explosive secret's about to be revealed…

TOO SMART FOR MARRIAGE Cathie Linz

Marriage Makers

Anastasia Knight vowed to teach David Sullivan how to have fun—he was far too serious! She and David together? No, they were both too smart for that…

0008/22a

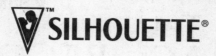

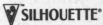

THE MACGREGORS

4 BOOKS ON THIS WELL-LOVED FAMILY

BY

NORA ROBERTS

*Don't miss these four fantastic books by
Silhouette's top author*

0002/115/SH4

FR
22

FREE!

2 Books
and a surprise gift!

We would like to take this opportunity to thank you for reading this Silhouette® book by offering you the chance to take TWO more specially selected titles from the Desire™ series absolutely FREE! We're also making this offer to introduce you to the benefits of the Reader Service™—

- ★ FREE home delivery
- ★ FREE gifts and competitions
- ★ FREE monthly Newsletter
- ★ Books available before they're in the shops
- ★ Exclusive Reader Service discounts

Accepting these FREE books and gift places you under no obligation to buy; you may cancel at any time, even after receiving your free shipment. Simply complete your details below and return the entire page to the address below. *You don't even need a stamp!*

YES! Please send me 2 free Desire books and a surprise gift. I understand that unless you hear from me, I will receive 4 superb new titles every month for just £2.70 each, postage and packing free. I am under no obligation to purchase any books and may cancel my subscription at any time. The free books and gift will be mine to keep in any case.

DOZEB

Ms/Mrs/Miss/Mr ....Initials ....

BLOCK CAPITALS PLEASE

Surname ....

Address ....

....

....Postcode ....

Send this whole page to:
UK: The Reader Service, FREEPOST CN81, Croydon, CR9 3WZ
EIRE: The Reader Service, PO Box 4546, Kilcock, County Kildare (stamp required)